Clarence Stanhope

In and Around Newport

1891 - A guide to the place showing where and how to see the most, in a

short time

Clarence Stanhope

In and Around Newport

1891 - A guide to the place showing where and how to see the most, in a short time

ISBN/EAN: 9783337192860

Printed in Europe, USA, Canada, Australia, Japan

Cover: Foto ©Andreas Hilbeck / pixelio.de

More available books at **www.hansebooks.com**

ESTABLISHED 1812.   INCORPORATED 1889.

DAVIS COLLAMORE & CO.,

LIMITED

Importers of

PORCELAIN,

POTTERY

AND

GLASS.

921 Broadway cor 21st. St. and 151 Fifth Avenue connecting

NEW YORK.

3 Casino Block.

NEWPORT, R. I.

F. W. MERRILL.

IMPORTER AND DEALER IN

ENGLISH AND AMERICAN SADDLERY,

STABLE OUTFITS,

Also in Connection with Harness Department,

TRUNKS, BAGS, ETC.,

118 Bellevue Avenue.

NEWPORT, R. I.

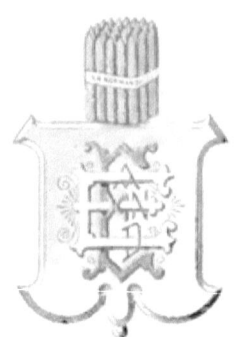

THE

AMERICAN

BOSTON,

Hanover, near Washington Street,

RUSSELL & STURGIS, PROPRIETORS.

Equally Desirable for Business or Pleasure.

WITH MEALS $3.00 PER DAY AND UPWARDS.

WITHOUT MEALS $1.00 PER DAY AND UPWARDS

According to Location of Rooms

Parlors and Baths Extra.

THE NEAREST FIRST-CLASS HOTEL TO EASTERN AND
NORTHERN DEPOTS.

ALSO PROPRIETORS OF

HOTEL WELLESLEY,

WELLESLEY, MASS.

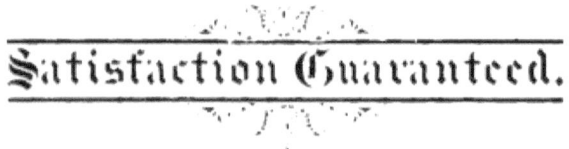

M. Steinert & Sons Co.

of Boston, Providence, New Haven and Cincinnati, Ohio

have opened their store in

Newport, R. I., for the season

on BELLEVUE AVE.

four doors north of Bath Road where all the styles

of the celebrated makes of the

STEINWAY & SONS, WEBER,

HARDMAN, ERNEST GABLER & BRO,

PEASE & HENNING

Grand and Upright Pianos can be seen.

Century & Smvetta.

S. JACOB

COLONIAL FURNITURE.

China, Books, Engravings and Arms.

SOUTH SEA ISLAND AND INDIAN RELICS.

SHELLS, MINERALS AND FOSSILS.

10, 12 & 14 BELLEVUE, NEWPORT, R. I.

And 6 Beacon Street, BOSTON, Mass.

KAULL & ANTHONY.

MARKET AND GROCERY,

---

301 and 303 Thames St.,

NEWPORT. R. I.

T. FRED KAULL.   CHAS. C. ANTHONY.

HAYWARD'S

~ LIVERY STABLES ~

Downing Street,

NEWPORT. R. I.

Horses, Carriages and Harnesses of Every Description for Sale or to Let, for Season or Single Trip.

Horses and Carriages taken for Winter

FOR STORAGE AND BOARD.

SCANNEVIN & POTTER,

ELECTRICAL ENGINEERS

— AND —

CONTRACTORS.

Estimates Furnished for ELECTRICAL WORK of All Descriptions.
Prompt Attention Given Repairs and Alterations

Agents for Electric Motors of all Kinds.

OFFICE: Southwest corner of Mill and Thames Sts.

ADDRESS ORDERS P. O. BOX 96,

NEWPORT, R. I.

CHAS. F. FRASCH,

. . . .

CONFECTIONER

170 THAMES STREET,

NEWPORT. R. I.

FINE CHINA. **ART POTTERY.**

Higgins & Seiter.

HIGH CLASS CHINA FROM ALL THE
LEADING POTTERIES OF THE WORLD AT
STRICTLY MODERATE PRICES. NOVEL-
TIES CONSTANTLY BEING RECEIVED.

170 BELLEVUE AVE.,

NEWPORT, R. I.

Branch of

50 & 52 W. 22ND ST., N. Y.

RICH CUT GLASS. **WEDDING GIFTS.**

EVERETT HOUSE,

17th and FOURTH AVENUE, NEW YORK,

Overlooking the beautiful grounds of Union Square, especially adapted,

on account of its cool location, for summer guests,

J. G. Weaver, Jr., & Co.,

Proprietors.

OCEAN HOUSE,

Adjoining Casino Grounds, Newport, R. I.

Three Concerts daily by the Celebrated Hungarian Band.

First Class Livery Stable, Carriages of all Descriptions to be had

on Application at Hotel Office.

J. G. Weaver, Jr.,

22

George E. Vernon & Co.,

Manufacturers and Dealers in

MODERN & ANTIQUE FURNITURE.

Old Dutch and English Silver.

Upholstering in all its Branches.

91 JOHN ST., NEWPORT, R. I.

H. N. HASSARD & CO.,

SOLE AGENTS FOR THE

HYGEIA

Sparkling Distilled Water Co.

Wholesale and Retail Dealers in all Kinds of Mineral Spring Waters.

164 BELLEVUE AVE., NEWPORT, R. I.

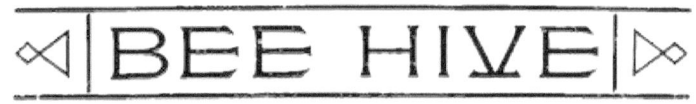

Tents of all Sizes Rented, Lighted and Decorated.

Piazzas Enclosed with White Striped Canvas and Turkey Red.

CAMP, DINING CHAIRS AND TABLES RENTED.

WITH RUGS OF ALL SIZES

Japanese and Teakwood Lanterns, Japanese Umbrellas and Various Decorations of every description. Piano, Bouquet, Brass and Silver Table Lamps rented at reasonable terms.

Reflecting Lights for Lawn and Carriage Runs. Lawn Illuminating Cups of all colors rented and arti-tically arranged.

A. C. LANDERS,

COVELL'S BLOCK, 167 THAMES ST.

1891.

A GUIDE TO THE PLACE, SHOWING WHERE AND HOW TO SEE THE
MOST, IN A SHORT TIME, WITH A LIST OF THE SUMMER
COTTAGERS, TABLE OF DISTANCES TO PROMI-
NENT PLACES, TIDE TABLE, CHURCH
DIRECTORY AND OTHER
INFORMATION.

By CLARENCE STANHOPE.

PREFACE.

In placing this book before the public we do so feeling that it will supply a long felt want of the cottager and tourist for a reliable guide to our beautiful city and its many attractions, and enable the cottager to locate their many friends. Great care has been taken to have the work as complete and reliable as it is possible to make it, so that it will meet the approbation of the public. In the description of various places we have combined enough of the past to make the present interesting, and is the result of many months' research among old records, etc. With so much by way of a preface; we leave the work to the tender mercies of our friends.

Respectfully,

CLARENCE STANHOPE.

INDEX TO CONTENTS.

ADVERTISERS' INDEX.

THE OLD STONE MILL.

CHAPTER I

N 1637 a number of colonists, whose idea of religious liberty was at variance with the dominant party of Massachusetts, were allowed for their own good to depart from the colony and settle elsewhere, and through the interposition of Roger Williams, who was on friendly terms with the Indians, Canonicus and Miantonomi, the chiefs of the tribes who inhabited the island at this time, were induced to sell for the nominal payment of forty fathoms of white beads and for a gratuity to the present inhabitants of ten coats and twenty hoes, the island of Aquidneck, which they transferred to William Coddington and his associates, and in 1638 Coddington and his followers settled on the north end of the island, at what is now Portsmouth. Owing to the rapid increase by newcomers among the settlers a number of them came to the south end of the island and establishing a new colony called it Newport. The following year the two colonies united held the first general court of election at Newport and elected William Coddington their governor. Under the wise administration of Governor Coddington the colony prospered, land was divided among the settlers, and the tilling of the soil begun for the means of sustenance. The following year they established the first public school and began the education of the youth among them. In 1643 Providence (which had previously been settled by Roger Williams), Portsmouth and Newport were incorporated by the Commissioners of Parliament under the name of " Incorporation of Providence Plantations in the Narragansett Bay

in New England," and a year later the name of the island was changed from "Aquidneck" to "the Isle of Rhodes or Rhode Island." We will not follow the settlers in their struggle for a livelihood, but the indomitable courage of the colony surmounted the difficulties as they presented themselves, and step by step they rose to the pinnacle of success, and had the most successful colony yet established in the new world. In 1760 Newport was at her height of prosperity. During the months of July and August of this year there arrived at this port sixty-four vessels from foreign voyages, seventeen whalemen and one hundred and thirty-four coasters, and for the next few months there were sixteen cargoes of molasses landed, comprising over three thousand hogsheads. All these vessels were owned by the merchants of the city and their cargoes were imported for manufacturing purposes, but the high rate of taxation imposed by the British authorities became unbearable, and the first overt act of violence was offered to the British authorities in America on the 10th of July, 1769, when the British revenue sloop Liberty was destroyed in our harbor. Of course the authority of the home government could not be trifled with and the colonists must be made to feel that they were indebted to the British home rule for their very existence. Other vessels were sent to this country bringing people with greater power and authority to subjugate the colonists, but being imbued with the true spirit of the "Sons of Liberty" they rebelled, and in June, 1775 the first naval engagement of the Revolution occurred in the outer harbor between a colonial sloop commanded by Captain Abraham Whipple, and a tender of the British frigate Rose, in which the tender was chased on to Conanicut shore and captured. In less than a year the General Assembly formally renounced allegiance to Great Britain, and a few weeks later, by a vote taken, formally approved of the Declaration of Independence. This was too much for the British authorities to stand, and in December, 1776, a large British fleet arrived, commanded by Sir Peter Parker, with an army of 10,000 men, English and Hessians, who made the inhabitants captive and began their work of devastation. Churches, public buildings and private residences were used for all sorts of purposes, and the inhabitants forced to provide for the invaders. All kinds of indignities were heaped upon the people and the commerce of the place ruined. In July, 1778, the French fleet, consisting of eleven ships of the line, besides frigates and transports, under command of Count D'Estaing, arrived off the town and caused consternation among the British soldiers who were quartered on the Island until the fall of 1779, when a fleet of fifty-two sail arrived and took off 7,000 men with all their ordnance and military stores, and evacuated the town, cutting down trees, burning warehouses and wharves and destroying everything in reach, taking with them all of the public records and other valuable property, and sailed for other fields to carry on their depredations. In the summer following the departure of the British from this place, another French fleet of forty-four sail, under Admiral De Ternay, arrived with 6,000 French troops, who were to become the allies of the Americans, and it was while they were here that General Washington, who was in command of the American army, made his first visit to Newport, and was received by the inhabitants with a perfect ovation. Newport as a commercial port never recovered from the blow received by the invasion of the British forces and the ruthless destruction of the property of its enterprising merchants. At one time it was the largest port of entry on the Atlantic coast, having its vessels in all parts of the world, some engaged in human traffic on Africa's coast, exchanging rum and other commodities for human beings to be sold into slavery; others hunting the leviathans of the deep, and at this time it was a large manufacturing town, having its many oil and candle factories, distilleries, sugar refineries, rope walks, ship-yards (where most of its vessels were built), large furniture factories and many other industries, and the products of all these manufactures were shipped to New York, the West Indies and other places, but the hand of time has been laid upon this, and the former industries of the place have given way to the entertainment of the summer people who have made Newport their home during the best part of the year, and to them Newport owes its present prosperity. To its location and natural attractions and the substantial aid from the first families of the land it has grown from a town of 6,716 inhabitants in 1790 to its present size as a city of 19,500 population, with probably an increase of its resident population in summer to nearly 30,000. Through the forethought of our city fathers and the enterprise and encouragement of our sojourners, the inhabitants have gradually been drawn out of their old ruts, and, as it were, new life instilled in their veins, and now the people of the city are as progressive as in any place in the world, with but the one idea of making its attractions, natural and artificial, more attractive, and thus draw more of the wealth and culture of the country to its hospitable shores. Beautiful roads have been built by private enterprise through lands that were heretofore almost inaccessible, and land brought into market for the purchasers of homes who desire a quiet and picturesque spot to pass the summer days, and many elegant houses have been erected in places that were but a few years ago wild and barren. Newport is more than favored in its historical connections, and among its older inhabitants the treasures of the past are carefully cherished, and as they are passing away all too fast, the present generation should be educated to take their place and keep alive the spirit of our forefathers who fought for their country and their homes that we of the present generation might enjoy the freedom and liberty of the present day. Of the historical connections of various parts of the place we will treat in the following pages, and tell the visitor, who has but a few hours to spare in the city, how the most can be seen in a short time.

CHAPTER II.

IF ARRIVING by boat or cars a carriage can be engaged at a reasonable sum for the ten-mile drive, so called, and starting from the **Parade or Washington Square**, by the Mall, where will be seen the statue of Commodore Oliver Hazard Perry, "the hero of Lake Erie," dedicated to his memory on September 10th, 1885, the seventy-second anniversary of the battle of Lake Erie, and representing the hero as he appeared at the time of gaining the deck of the brig Niagara, after leaving his shattered flagship Lawrence. The statue is the work of William G. Turner, a native of the place, was cast in one piece at Florence, Italy, and cost $15,000. It was paid for by the State, which contributed one-half, the city one-third and private subscription of one-sixth, while almost opposite, in the building whose lower story is occupied as a market, was the residence of the hero. Beyond is seen the open square, known as the **Parade** where have been enacted some of the most important events in the history of Newport, and with its old **State House**, built about 1738-43, in which once a year the inauguration of Rhode Island's chief magistrate takes place and is duly announced from the balcony over its main entrance with its old-time custom of informing the people gathered on the street below with its "Hear ye! hear ye!" etc., and closing with the words, "and God save the State of Rhode Island and Providence Plantations for the year ensuing." Continuing up Touro street we come to the **Jews' Synagogue,** where some of the most prominent Jews of America worship, for to them Newport owes much of her prosperity. On the lot adjoining the synagogue is the home of the **Newport Historical Society,** where can be found historical lore and implements of warfare, as well as the more peaceful utensils of domestic use, all bearing testimony to the long ago. The building itself is a very old one, and was for many long years the house of worship for those of the Sabbatarian faith, more familiarly known as the Seventh Day Baptists, and is one of two churches in the city whose sacredness was not desecrated by the British when they occupied the town. This building was purchased a few years ago by the Historical Society and moved to its present location. Passing up the street we come to the residence of G. M. Tooker; on the left at the corner of Kay street, and on the opposite corner is the **Jews' Cemetery,** where lie the remains of some of Newport's early

and prominent Hebrews, and which place has been made the theme of the poet Longfellow. Here Touro street ends and Bellevue Avenue begins. On the right is the residence of R. M. Hunt, and at the corner of the street adjoining is the **Newport Reading Room,** where the more conservative of the summer residents can enjoy a quiet club life. A short distance beyond on the left is

Redwood Library, established in 1747, through the munificence of Abraham Redwood in his day, and many others with the same generosity who have acted their part on the stage of life and have left rich stores of literature for the use of coming generations. On the right we come to a large opening known as **Touro Park**. It is here that the world famous "**Old Stone Mill**" stands, which has been the theme for poets and literary men, but with the research of antiquarians its origin is no nearer solution to-day than it was a hundred years ago. Pages could be written on this subject without exhausting the theme, but we will leave it and speak again on the subject. On this square stands the statue erected to the memory of Matthew Calbraith Perry, who was the first naval officer to open up the commercial relations that now exist between the United States and Japan. On the street to the south and facing the park is the **Channing Memorial Church**, dedicated October 10, 1881, to the memory of William Ellery Channing. Continuing down the avenue we come to the **Newport Casino**, erected in 1880 by James Gordon

Bennett, and who still owns (but does not occupy) the stone villa directly opposite. The Casino is owned by a corporation composed of the wealthiest of Newport's summer residents, among whom are

millionaires without number. It is used as a resort for the entertainment of its patrons and has a private club connected with it for its gentlemen members, and it is here that the elite of society daily congregate to listen to the delightful music or to talk over the latest society news. A short distance beyond is the **Ocean House**, Newport's famous hostelry, which is managed by the same parties who have made its name and reputation famous. Continuing by this place we see the villa on the right owned by the Duchess de Dino with the summer house of Samuel F. Barger adjoining, and on the opposite corner is the residence of Col. C. L. Best. Directly opposite on the left is the villa of G. G. Haven, with that of William G. Weld of Boston near by with its granite walls and brown stone trimmings setting off its beauty. Opposite on the right is the villa of Mrs. S. T. Swan of Baltimore, occupying most of the lawn for its solid foundation. A few minutes driving brings us to Narragansett Avenue, where on the left-hand corner is the residence of C. C. Baldwin with its quaint cream-colored walls, and on the opposite corner is the granite stone house of William H. Osgood of New York. Directly opposite is the colony of fine residences owned by Mrs. Mary A. C. Holmes of Boston, and on the same side follow the villas of Mrs. Merrill and that of Wm. Starr Miller, with that of Mrs. J. F. Stone adjoining. The brick house that we see on the left with its picturesque surroundings is owned by J. M. Hodgson the florist, and is occupied by Sidney Webster, and a little farther on the right, secluded from the gaze of passersby, is the residence of Mrs. Whiting. Following on the same side is the Bruen villa, and beyond on the farther corner of the by-street is the residence of Mrs. John Carter Brown of Providence, who has for a neighbor Walter L. Kane in the adjoining enclosure, while directly opposite is the fine stone mansion of Rhode Island's ex-governor, George Peabody Wetmore, surrounded by its many acres of well-kept lawn and shade trees of great variety and rarity, all enclosed by its neat granite wall, whose height does not forbid the visitor to look upon one of the finest places in Newport. Adjoining, with its low brick wall,

surmounted by a wooden coping, is the place which once contained the home of James R. Keene which was destroyed by fire December

31st, 1886, and the property has since been in the market for sale. A short distance beyond and in view from the avenue is the home of

Wm. Watts Sherman of New York. On the left, with its low ivy-clad wall, is the villa of John W. Ellis, and on the next corner is the villa formerly owned by Vice-President L. P. Morton, but now the

property of I. Townsend Burden, while on the right diagonal corner is the picturesque villa of William Storrs Wells with its tower and gables surmounted with a handsome finial. Still continuing, we pass the residence of the late August Belmont on our left, while on the right looms up the immense structure of Theo. A. Havemeyer, and turning our eyes to the left again we see the villa of Mrs. William Astor, known as "Beechwood," and next, in process of construction, is the magnificent marble palace of William K. Vanderbilt. Adjacent to this is the villa of W. W. Astor, on the same side, while on the opposite side of the avenue and facing the low granite wall which makes the western boundary of Dr. C. M. Bell's imposing brick structure, are the cottages of the Swift heirs, N. C. Thayer and Mrs. J. J. Post. Again on the left is the villa of Thomas F. Cushing with its pretty rustic fence, and opposite are the villas of Mrs. J. T. Gilbert and E. L. Winthrop. As we make the turn in the avenue, on the left and beyond the dense mass of trees is the residence of F. W. Vanderbilt, which we will notice in another chapter. Still on the left and quite close to old ocean is the home of H. H. Cook, and next to this is the new villa of H. M. Brooks. On the right as we turned the avenue we passed Gen. J. F. Pierson's villa, and beyond we see the neat and pretty stone structure called "Inchiquin," built by Mr. J. O'Brien for his daughter, Mrs. C. F. Livermore, but we are at the end of Bellevue avenue and facing **Bailey's Beach,** which is fast becoming the proper place for bathing by the summer residents. A stone wall placed across what was once the driveway to the beach bars further progress, so we will make a detour and continue our drive along the road skirting the beach. We are now upon **Ocean Avenue,** or as more commonly called Ocean drive. Passing by the beach and situated on the rocky headland at our left is a large cavity in the rocks known as the **"Spouting Rock,"** where old ocean, after a heavy southeast storm, rolls in with its mighty waves, and, filling the cavity, will force the water into the air to the heighth of fifty feet or more, presenting to the fortunate visitor a scene of sublime grandeur. Here is situated but a little way from the sea the summer home of Henry Clews, while near by is the house of R. M. Cushing. Going up the short hill and turning to the left we go by one of the many houses owned by J. N. A. Griswold, and in the distance, situated on **Gooseberry Island,** may be seen the club house of the Newport Fishing Club, whose membership comprises many of our summer residents. We will here diverge from our trip and give a little bit of history connected with this island, but little known. When the original settlers divided the land among the inhabitants there were many goring pieces which were left, and afterward these irregular pieces were apportioned to the several settlers. After the apportionments had been made it was found that one Col. John Cranston had been overlooked, and as this island had not been given to anyone it was voted at a meeting of the committee for the ordering the laying out of the undivided land of said town, held March 24, 1713-14, as follows : "Whereas Col. John Cranston never had any land laid out him in his right of commonage to his home and land according to the acts as others had, therefore we order and agree that s'd Cranston shall have a rock or island lying on the south side of Rhode Island, called Gooseberry Island, in full of his right, which island lyeth over against Jaheel Brenton Esqr's land, formerly Mews Farme to be to s'd Cranston in his right to him and his heirs and assigns forever," since which time it passed from one heir to another through more than a century, until the last rightful owner sold it in 1847 to Messrs. Wm. Glennan, John H. Crosby and John Beattie, and this last deed of the island is the only one on record, although the island is claimed by and the rents of the same are paid to the Newport Hospital, who were bequeathed the same, together with other lands adjoining, by the late owner, Gen. J. A. Hazard, and as it stands to-day it is quite a valuable piece of property, and its rightful ownership would be a question for the courts to settle as there is no deed to be found on record other than the one of 1847. But we will not delay the visitor longer and so continue our ride. After crossing the bridge spanning the tide way we will see two cottages close together near the shore, where Theo W. and Jerome C. Borden pass their summer days, while beyond we have in view the building surmounted by a tower that is the quarters of the crew of the **United States Life-Saving Service**, situated on the headland known as Price's Neck. The next point of interest that we will meet will be the sight of a headstone lying between the roadway and the ocean, where lie the remains of two unknown sailors whose bodies were washed ashore many years ago and were interred close by the place where found, and since then this headland has been known as "Graves Point." Continuing on we go by the place selected by J. R. Busk for a summer home and where the workmen are busily engaged in its construction. The next villa is Theo. M. Davis's, and right here it will be well to stop and gaze upon old ocean, where its tumultuous waves are forever breaking upon the reef that makes out from the land for a long distance and is known as **Brenton's Reef**, while at the outer end of the reef is moored the lightship, to warn the mariner of the danger lurking beneath the white-capped waves. Continuing our journey we pass the villa of Ross R. Winans, known as "Bleak House," and still keeping the ocean in view we go by the villa of Professor Agassiz in the distance and close to the shore on the headland of **Castle Hill**. Presently we pass the residence of Josiah O. Low and next adjoining that of A. A. Low. Turning abruptly to the right we leave old ocean behind us, and after passing the residence of J. W. Auchincloss on the left we soon catch a glimpse of Newport harbor by looking across **Brenton's Cove**, where will be seen at low water the wrecks of three vessels that have made the cove their final haven, one of which, the "Bessie Rogers," has been utilized by E. D. Morgan as a boat house close by his elegant mansion, situated just above, on the high rocks, which commands one of the finest views on the island, with the harbor below and Narragansett Bay stretching to the northward as far as the eye can reach, while to our right on the hill will be seen the villa of J. B. and Miss Grosvenor of Providence as well as that of G. G. King; continuing along the road we pass many of the older and less pretensious cottages until we approach Halidon avenue; turning to the left we pass the villa of **Mrs. Schuyler Hamilton Jr.**, on the right and descend the hill where through the opening of the arching trees we see a cluster of rocks a short distance from the shore with a snow white house perched upon them, which is a government lighthouse and keeper's dwelling

known as the **Lime Rock Lighthouse,** watched over by the eagle eye of Ida Lewis the "Grace Darling of America;" turning to the right we pass along the road skirting the harbor and by the residences on the hill above us, of F. O. French, Lorillard Spencer and Mrs. E. G. Hartshorn and soon reach Thames street, the principal business thoroughfare of the city. Driving rapidly up the street, by its old and antiquated buildings, past the shot tower and lead works, and the old Aquidneck Mill, we soon reach the Perry Mill all sorry reminders of Newport's former manufacturing days, and a short distance beyond on the right is the Post Office and Custom House with the Stars and Stripes above. We are now in the midst of the business places of Newport's merchant's and more modern buildings are to be seen. By the wharves and narrow streets we hasten and soon pass on the left, on the corner of Long Wharf, a low antiquated brick building which is the City Hall of America's famous watering place. Turning abruptly to the right we are once more at our starting point the Parade, and our ten mile drive is a thing of the past.

CHAPTER III.

SHOULD the visitor desire to see more of the splendid mansions of the wealthy, a short drive can be had by passing over a part of Bellevue Avenue again until **Narragansett Avenue** is reached, when, turning to the left we approach the cottage of Mrs. G. Tiffany on the left, with that of G. H. Warren adjoining on the opposite corner and with those of E. H. Schemerhorn, Mrs. W. F. Weld and Miss Callender adjoining respectively, while across the way are to be seen the villas of C. N. Fay with that of R. T. Wilson adjoining. The cluster of dark painted houses are the Pinard Cottages, on the opposite corner is the residence of F. Sheldon, while across the way is the villa of Mrs. M. L. Travers. Continuing along the avenue we go by the residence of Col. G. R. Fearing which is situated some distance from the roadway surrounded by a large number of beautiful trees and is known as "The Orchard;" adjoining are the villas of R. I. Gammell and Mrs. Wm. Gammell of Providence. We are now at the end of the avenue and at the well known place called " **Forty Stops**," which has recently been improved, artificially, by the erection of a substantial platform overlooking the rocks below; retracing our way we go by the brick mansion of Robert Goelet, and turning down the first road to the left enter upon **Ochre Point Avenue** and pass the villa of Ogden Goelet in construction, and the Pendleton cottage adjacent. On our right, surrounded by a high and massive stone wall is the beautiful stone villa of J. J. Van Alen, known as "Wakehurst," while on the opposite side is

the summer home of Louis L. Lorillard, bequeathed to him by the late Miss Wolfe, while on the right we pass the Acosta Cottages, and beyond, on the same side, is the handsome stone structure of J. J. Wysong and the Eldredge villa adjoining on the farther corner. On the left and hidden by the dense mass of foliage, is the villa of Cornelius Vanderbilt. We now turn to the right on to Ruggles

Avenue, going by Fairman Rogers on the left, with that of Miss Jones and J. M. Fiske adjoining, while opposite is the villa of Prof. C. W. Shields, with that of J. T. Spencer's beyond; turning to the left we pass through a short by-street separating the two villas of J. P. Kersnochan, that on the left is known as "The Cloister." Turning to the right and we are upon Marine avenue and go by the residence of Gordon McKay on the right, while on the other side are the large and spacious grounds of the late August Belmont, extending from the avenue to the cliffs, continuing a short distance and we reach Bellevue Avenue again, and turn to the right pass over the avenue to our starting place. Should the visitor chance to take this drive in the afternooon a grand opportunity will be had of seeing the magnificent turnouts of wealth and fashion in their daily afternoon outing on Newport's famous avenue. We will now leave you to amuse yourself until we prepare for another trip which must be done part of the way on foot.

CHAPTER IV.

HOULD the tourist start early in the morning, that is not later than 10 o'clock, or in the afternoon about 4 o'clock, taking the street car or one of the many drags plying between the avenue and the beach, a short ride will bring us to the foot of the road leading to the beach, or more properly speaking, Easton's Beach, the far-famed bathing place of America's Queen of Watering places, Newport; but we will not speak of its advantages at present. Alighting from the car or drag at the foot of the hill we will begin our tramp **along**

the Cliffs. The first villa we approach after entering on the wind-

ing path, is the Chanler villa, and then come to what is known as
the Cliff Cottages, the wants of whose tenants are supplied from
the main house or hotel. A short distance beyond are another
cluster of cottages known as the Livingston's. After passing them
we have quite a stretch of ground to cover until we come near to the
beautiful stone residence of Mrs. Wm. Gammell, and crossing the
boundary line of her enclosure we commence our tramp through
the spacious grounds and well kept lawn, and obeying the request
as given to us by the many signs placed along the walk "keep off
the grass" we now approach the "Forty Steps," where we find a
substantial stairway leading to the rocks below, or enter on the
platform overlooking the rocks, and gaze seaward. Directly opposite us on the headland may be seen the villa of Mrs. Z. C. Deas,
at Easton's Point and still farther beyond will be seen the hazy
outline of Sachuest Point, and still following, as the sun goes, will
be seen in the extreme distance West Island and lighthouse, while
beneath us on our right is a chain of rocks making out from the
mainland, known as "**Ellison's Rock**," where excellent fishing may
be had at the proper tide; leaving this spot we enter the enclosure
of Robert Goelet; passing through his grounds we approach the
elegant palace of his brother Ogden Goelet, with its many mullioned
windows, balconies and broad piazzas. We are now abreast of
the original "Forty Steps," whose old rickety stairway led to the
little beach below and where at the foot of the cliffs, long since ob-
literated by the angry waves, was one of the old time famous tryst-
ing places known as "**Conrade Cave**," and could the rocks speak
many a tale could it tell of the "plighting of the troth" of youth-
ful lovers. Resuming our walk we pass the less pretentious Pendleton Cottage; a few steps more and we are within the enclosure
of Louis L. Lorillard's, formerly known as Miss Wolfe's summer
residence, with its broad lawns and rare plants, and its natural attractions and the beach at the foot of the frowning cliffs makes it
the most picturesque spot along the cliffs; while in the distance and
adjoining this enclosure is to be seen the villa of Cornelius Van-

deridit. We are now upon the eastern or water side of Newport's summer colony known as **Ochre Point** and almost all
the land which is in view was the home of the American jurist,
Wm. Beach Lawrence who died in 1881. All this vast territory,
consisting of 69 acres, was bought by him previous to 1850, for
$12,000, and the last sale from the plat was the old homestead,
which was sold to Miss Wolfe for $102,000, and which she had torn
down to make room for a fine building. Passing through this enclosure to the next we go by the Vanderbilt villa, with its rustic
summer house on the left and steps leading to the shore below, and
approach the southernmost boundary of Ochre Point, a name given
to this part of Newport from the fact that the soil of the cliffs contained more or less of the substance. The villa we now approach is
the Pearson villa, and that of Fairman Rogers adjacent, who has
Miss Jones as a neighbor; and next is that of Josiah M. Fiske.
Leaving the "Cloister," one of J. P. Kernochan's houses, on the
right, we cross the foot of Marine avenue, passing through the turn-
stile and go by a rustic summer house on the left, enter upon the
walk skirting the spacious grounds of the late August Belmont, and
approach the famous rose garden of the late historian, George Ban-
croft, surrounded on its water side with a high hedge, at either end
of which is a pathway leading up into the grounds, and among the
immense variety of roses which were the delight of its former
owner, and many a visitor will live with the remembrance of having
received a flower from the hands of the aged historian. We now go
by the house of John Knower and approach the villa of Mrs. William Astor and by the marble palace of William K. Vanderbilt,
which is situated a short distance from the cliffs, and pass through
the grounds of W. W. Astor, and as the path rounds the cove, at the
base beneath us we see the boathouse situated on what is known as
"Sheep Point." Going by the residences of Mrs. Ingersoll and G.
W. Wales, we pass down the series of steps and are on the premises
of Dr. C. M. Bell, whose brick villa is above us on the higher land,
passing by a cave guarded by an iron barred door, the imagination

of the tourist must not be carried back to the days of the bold buc-
caneers, when Captain Kidd buried his wealth along the coast for
safety, and this cave as it appears, is but a short passage leading
from the house above. Continuing on our way we go by the residences of Ogden Mills and Thomas F. Cushing and approach the
long and picturesque stone mansion of F. W. Vanderbilt. On our
left can be seen the angry waves of the Atlantic breaking with a
roar upon what is known as "Rough Point." Just before we get
abreast of the house, and passing close to the headland, we go over
an artificial bridge which will not be known by the visitor unless
attention should be called to the fact. An illustration of this
bridge is given on our outside cover. Continuing our journey we go
by the residence of H. H. Cook with that of H. M. Brooks, and the
Sand's villa adjacent. We now pass through the gateway on to the
roadway leading from Bellevue avenue to the water, or more properly speaking, "Land's End." This place is better known as the
boat house landing, from the fact that until within a few years
there stood close to this place a one room stone building erected
soon after the great gale of 1815 by popular subscription to take
the place of the one swept away during this gale, and this shelter
was used principally by the fishermen who would go outside of the
reef for his daily fare; but the land changing ownership this old
landmark was torn down, and a short distance beyond a wooden
tower was erected, from the top of which a fine view can be had for
the trouble of ascending the winding stairway. The huge mass of
rocks in front of us and a short distance from the mainland is
"Coggeshall's Ledge," and the cove or harbor which this ledge pro-
tects from the fury of the ocean storms is known as Boathouse
Gully, and here at the right time can be found the hardy fisherman
whose boats may be seen drawn up on the shore, who for a proper
consideration will take you out for a fishing excursion beyond the
reef, where the follower of Izaak Walton can enjoy deep sea fishing
to his heart's content. We will not linger here, but passing through
the gateway on the opposite side of the road continue our way over

the hill and by the tower, approaching the villa of Mrs. Richard Baker, and those adjoining and along the paths skirting the shore of the eastern boundary of **Bailey's Beach** with its long row of bath houses all under one roof, with its short tower in the centre as a sort of guard over its lower structure, we pass out and are once more upon Bellevue avenue, where a drag can be found that will take us homeward, and by the homes of those through whose grounds we have just passed and our cliff walk is ended.

CHAPTER V.

UR next trip we will make to Easton's Beach,
taking a drag or the street car a few minutes drive
will bring us to our destination. The beach at the
time Newport was settled and the land divided
among the settlers fell to the lot of Nicholas
Easton and was utilized in its early days for its sand and seaweed
privileges, but the mark of improvement is as noticeable here as
elsewhere in our ancient city, where a few years ago the bath houses
were roughly constructed affairs with wooden wheels upon them
and covered with a thin coat of whitewash, forming quite a contrast
with the present well constructed long, low and rambling building
erected in 1887 at a cost of over $50,000, with its wings extending
on either side of the main building wherein are the modern bath
houses with other rooms adjacent where hot and cold salt water
baths can be enjoyed, and its well supplied restaurant where one
can enjoy a simple shore dinner, its broad covered piazza where pro-
tected from the sun's scorching rays one can sit and watch the antics
of the bathers, or the eye can gaze upon the ocean and watch the
ever passing vessels in the distance as they sail to and fro, while
upon the right stretches the cliffs with their beautiful villas and
emerald lawns which we saw in our walk a short time ago, while on
the left and close to the water's edge at the farther end of the beach
lies the colony of cottages belonging to the Newport Land Company,
and which are managed after the same manner as the Pinard and
Cliff cottages, while on the extreme point of land may be seen the
villa owned by Mrs. Z. C. Deas, and situated on what is known as

Easton's Point. If inclined, a plunge into the water can be made
after changing our garments and donning a suit of clothes that
can be hired at the office of the main building, resting assured that
the beach is perfectly safe and with but little undertow notwith-

standing the patrol which is kept up by the men in the boat, which
precaution is taken to guard against any accident to the more ven-
turesome bathers who often swim out beyond the farthest breaker
and then swim in again on the top of the breakers, somewhat after
the style of the surf bathers of the Sandwich Islands, minus the
board. But few accidents have happened on this famous beach, and
then the result was more from the carelessness of the bathers than
from any other cause. **The fashionable hour for bathing** is
from 11 to 12 o'clock, and after one o'clock for a couple of hours the
beach is given up principally to men, but during the hour first mentioned the beach is the scene of great animation and gaiety and
the striking costumes of the fair bathers is wonderful and bewilder-
ing with the many gay hues and exquisite taste manifested by the
wearer to make beauty more beautiful. It is also a great gathering
place for the little ones who are carefully guarded by an older person
and with their little pails and shovel they dig in the sand to their
heart's content, or, if permission is obtained, they doff their shoes

and stockings to paddle in the water, when a tiny wave with force far spent surrounds them, the air will be filled with the laughter of the happy little ones.

History tells us that in 1750 a party of fishermen who were on the beach were surprised at seeing a large ship heading for shore but some distance away, carefully wending her way past the more dangerous places but still approaching, when all at once her headway stopped. Hastily launching a boat they put out to her and upon boarding the vessel, greatly to their surprise, not a living soul was to be seen and the ship's boat was gone somewhere with its living freight. Everything on board was in its proper place and a fire was burning briskly in the galley stove and the whereabouts of the captain and crew was and ever will be a mystery. The vessel was one that belonged to one of Newports merchants and was daily expected home with a rich cargo from foreign lands and was gotten off from the beach and taken to the harbor, where she was afterwards sold for the benefit of the wreckers. After refitting she made many successful voyages. It is but a few years ago that the brig Ida McLeod, laden with petroleum, came ashore and was gotten off with slight damage, and after repairs were made and her cargo reloaded she started again on her voyage, only to be overtaken again by the cruel hand of fate, and was fallen in with in mid-ocean, abandoned and waterlogged, but such cases as these are of great rarity. Let us now picture to our minds the scenes enacted here during some of the storms of winter, when but few people would venture to the place while the storm rages; then the smooth beach is torn up and gullies are formed, large stones lying beneath the sands are exposed to view and the wind and sea hold high carnival. From the eastermost point of the beach to the shore huge waves roll in in rapid succession with deafening roar, leaping and dashing, break close to the buildings, and still rushing on in mad career pass across the roadway into the pond beyond; while on the western or right hand side will strike angrily against the stone wall and leap into the air to the height of twenty feet or more, falling back again, only to be met by another incoming wave, and uniting with it as though in unity there is strength, strike the wall again as if bent on its destruction, while on the cliff side of the beach will be seen the white capped billow as

"The breaking waves dash high
On the stern and rock-bound coast."

After one of these storms and with a strong northwest wind and a shining sun, the scene is one of great beauty, as the huge waves roll high and are just about to break, the strong wind cuts the top of them, and as the fleecy spray is blown off, they show all the prismatic colors of the rainbow, in fact, numbers of small rainbows fill the air from the constant spray coming from the waves, and at such times as these the sight is worth travelling a long distance to witness. After the storm has subsided and the tide goes out, the fishermen, as well as others, reap a harvest and find a ready market for the beach clams which the ocean has so bountifully placed before them. But as the bathing hour is at an end, the carriages with their gay parties are rapidly passing up the hill again, and the beach is being forsaken for the cool shades of the pavilion piazzas, we will leave this delightful spot for fresher fields of observation.

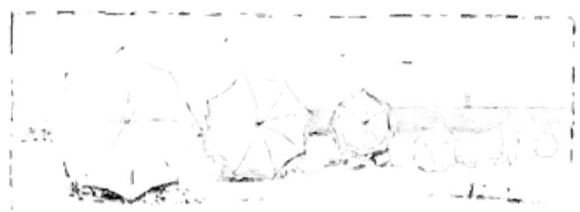

CHAPTER VI.

FOR our next trip we will engage a carriage at the Ocean House for a drive across the beaches and out on the island by way of the Indian Avenue drive which is best taken in the afternoon, passing rapidly down Bath Road and across Easton's Beach, by the Newport Land Company's cottages we begin the ascent of the long hill known as Purgatory Road, by the residence on the left of H. W. Bookstaver, W. H. Morrison and Julien T. Davies while on the opposite side is the villa of L. C. Josephs, we soon come to a turn in the road where we will stop and alight, passing through the opening in the fence we wend our way to the top of the short hill and going along the rocks soon come to a fissure in the rocks known as **Purgatory** whose origin is supposed to have been caused by the sudden upheaval of the earth in ages long ago when the earth was supposed to have been in a very heated condition, as the composition of the stone is what is known as pudding stone and the sudden cooling of the mass caused the separation which formed the place now seen. It is about 150 feet in length from the face of the cliffs to its land end, from 12 to 14 feet wide at its outward end. Until within a few years ago it was said to be bottomless, but careful soundings made have exploded this story and it is known to have a hard sandy bottom with a depth of 18 feet of water at low tide. Within its enclosure is a cave which is not easily accessible. It has several legends connected with it, one of which is to the effect that a lover was pleading with his sweetheart to name the day when they might be united for life and his lady told him that he did not love her as much as he ought and the lover called on Heaven to witness him as he replied, that to prove his devotion to her he would do any command she would give. Thinking to frighten him and at the same time test his devotion to her, she bade him as a proof of his assertion to jump the chasm. He hesitated, but drawing back for a instant, he started, the maiden seeing the recklessness of her

command tried to stop him, with a sudden spring he jumped, landing safely on the opposite side, and turning, bade the cruel hearted girl farewell forever. Thus she jeopardized the life of a lover to gratify a foolish whim and lost his love by so doing. Another and more ancient one is that of the Indian maiden who had slain her faithless lover "Hobomoko" and realizing her terrible act and while slowly pacing the rocks crying out in despair for him to return to her again, beheld the form of his Satanic majesty approaching her, who replied to her question as to whom he was, said, "I am Hobomoko!" and seizing the luckless maiden he dragged her across the rocks and lifting her up, jumped into "Purgatory," and to this day may be seen what are said to be the foot-prints of the evil one. Hard by, will be seen a small granite stone with the initials and date of A. G. L., Sept. 9, 1850, placed there to mark the spot where a son of the late William Beach Lawrence met his accidental death while on a gunning expedition. Retracing our steps we enter the carriage again and continue our trip down the short hill and along the roadway skirting the Second or Sachuest Beach. This beach is but little used as a bathing place as it is not considered as safe as Easton's beach. On our left may be seen the embankment of a storage reservoir of Newport's water supply, while beyond as we approach the rocks, is to be seen **Paradise Valley** which makes up between the two chains of rocks while at the nearest end of this mass of rocky headland at whose base is a deep recess which furnishes a retreat, is the far-famed **Hanging Rock** and it is here that Bishop Berkeley an eminent divine who came to this country in 1728, used to pass much of his time, and here he wrote his famous book the Minute Philosopher. Here it was that Smibert the artist was inspired to place on canvas the charming color of a Rhode Island sunset, and here the Rev. James Honyman an associate of Bishop Berkeley received the divine inspiration while writing his remarkable sermons delivered by him while rector of Trinity Church. Thus the place although in Middletown has a treble interest to Newporters. Turning to the left by this rocky headland and passing over another bridge we continue over the hill, always keeping the ocean in view, or more properly speaking, the Seaconnet river, we pass along the roadway know as **Indian Avenue** and ascend the rise of the hill, the Seaconnet River is before us and forms the eastern boundary of our island home. We soon come to the summer home of the tragedian Edwin Booth and called by him "Boothden," while at the water side may be seen a quaint mill somewhat after the style of those used in Holland. Leaving this villa behind we approach a picturesque little chapel constructed of stone, with its ivy clad walls and dedicated to the memory of Bishop Berkeley whom we have previously mentioned. Still journeying on with the river at our right we soon come to Peckham's Lane on our left, turning into this road we approach the end and turn to the right on to Wapping Road and continue along and by Braman's Lane and soon pass on our right the residence of the late Thomas R. Hazard, more familiarly known to the inhabitants of our island as "Shepard Tom." This place is known as **"Vaucluse,"** and was until the Revolutionary war the summer home of Metcalf Bowler, one of Newport's most enterprising and highly respected citizens, one whose memory is still kept fresh in the minds of some of Newport's older inhabitants who daily pass on Thames street, by the sight of two carved eagles which surmount the doorway of two business houses.

Still following this roadway we make a turn of the road and soon come out opposite the farm of Cornelius Vanderbilt, known as **"Oakland."** Mr. Vanderbilt does not live here himself, but the farm is kept simply to supply his table with fresh products of the dairy and garden, and he makes almost daily visits to the place. The stock on the farm is of the purest breed and everything about the place is of the best, and all together is the finest fancy farm on the island. If time is plenty we can turn to the right and continue our ride on the island a little farther, and turning down the first road on the right come to the most beautiful and picturesque spot on the island, known as **"The Glen,"** although in former days it was known as "Cundall's Mill," and on this spot as late as 1811 Joseph Cundall, Esq., formerly a judge of the Supreme Court, was engaged in the manufacture of woollen goods, until he unfortunately perished during a very violent snow storm in December of that year, and whose body was not found for many days afterwards. Its present owner, H. A. C. Taylor, was a fortunate man when he became its owner, and through his enterprise the land has been brought to a high state of cultivation and the farm stocked with the purest bred cattle that money could purchase and the farm made what it is, another one of the fancy farms of the island. While retaining many of its old-time features, the grove of sturdy oaks, its old water mill and the ever gurgling brook which rushes madly over the stones and finds its way to the East river, if his good fortune to get a peep into the place the visitor will see a spot of rare beauty on our island home. Retracing our way and going by "Oakland," again keeping the road to the right down Turner's lane a short distance, we turn into the first road at our right, and then again to the left at the next, and once more to the right at the next road, we are upon Berkeley avenue, which will take us past the former home of Bishop Berkeley, known as **"Whitehall,"** situated a short distance from the road and partly hidden by the old orchard on our right. Here is the farm that was bequeathed to Yale College for the perpetual encouragement of classical learning, and the income derived from the rent of the farm was to help defray the expense of any student who passed the required examination, and in 1761 the farm, containing about 100 acres, was leased for a thousand years at a rental which brings the college less than two hundred dollars annually, and since the original lease was made it has changed hands many times. Continuing to the end of this road we come to Honyman Hill road, down which we pass by the summer residence of S. H. Witherbee and go quickly over the wooden bridge with the broad expanse of water on our left, which is the main source of supply of Newport's needs, up the steep hill by **Hillside Farm**, and a few minutes more brings us to its summit and we go by the villas of A. Van Rensselaer and H. Hoppin on the right, while on the left are those of W. C. Simms, Col. Prince and H. W. Willard adjoining, with that of R. N. Hazard on the corner and the imposing mansion of Major Bull on the right hand opposite corner. We are now at the "Mile corner," or in other words at the northern boundary of the city of Newport, which at this point is the terminus of the street car route. Turning to the left and passing along for a short distance we turn to the right down the first road and soon approach an imposing brown stone structure known as **"Malbone,"** the home of ex-Mayor Bedlow. It is here

that in 1742 Colonel Godfrey Malbone, a wealthy merchant of Newport, erected an elegant mansion on the spacious grounds with a
garden of many acres, wherein were the choicest fruit trees that
could be found in Europe, which were imported for his garden. In
the war of 1740 between France and Spain he fitted out several
private armed vessels of war, which made many important captures.
In the summer of 1766, while preparations were being made for a
dinner party, to be given to a number of distinguished people, the
house caught fire and was entirely destroyed. Mr. Malbone died in
1768 and was buried in a vault under Trinity Church. Later the

property came into the hands of J. Prescott Hall and another fine
mansion was erected, and afterwards it was purchased by the present
owner. Turning to the left we pass along this roadway and come
out again on Broadway, opposite Bliss road, which only a few years
ago was considered as being out in the country, but the rapid progress made and the large increase in the city's permanent population, the place has built up rapidly, and here are seen the homes of
many of Newport's successful merchants. Still continuing our journey down this broad street, and, by the way, its former name was
Broad street, until within a few years, when its name was changed

to the present one to meet the ideas of its more aspiring citizens, under the arching trees, by some of its older houses, and soon we pass the ancient State House and are on the Parade or Washington Square and turn down Thames street, with its bustling activity, and here we will leave you.

CHAPTER VII.

E will make our next trip to the Point, or as often called by many writers "Oldport". We will start from the Parade and journey down the delapidated water street known as **Long Wharf,** where are situated most of the boat shops in which many of Newports famous catboats are built during the long and tedious winters which must necessarily elapse after our summer visitors have departed. We soon come to a small bridge spanning an opening between the harbor and cove where the tide has ebbed and flowed for over two hundred years and here we stop and speak of its former scenes of activity. In the early days of the place the cove covered an area of many acres but since the introduction of the railroad it has been rapidly filled up for business purposes. During the height of Newport's commercial activity a large part of its interest lay in this vicinity and here in the cove of olden time there were seven wharves where vessels were constantly discharging their cargoes of molasses and other merchandise and reloading with a cargo of rum from the eleven distilleries that were in full operation, which was taken to the coast of Africa. There exchanged for slaves and other products of the coast and then again there were several shipyards where many vessels were built, and all the vessels had to pass through the drawbridge which at that time was twenty-six feet wide. In 1702 Long Wharf, which was built principally of wood, was called the

Old Town Wharf and was damaged by a severe gale, efforts were made to rebuild it, and the town council voted to let certain persons who offered to rebuild and keep it in order, have the control of it and collect the rents to reimburse themselves for the outlay and in 1750 under certain conditions the wharf was lengthened by the trustees, and seven years later authority was obtained from the General Assembly to maintain a ferry between Newport and Jamestown, and in 1760 the wharf suffered from a disastrous fire and unusual high tides and the General Assembly was asked for a grant to

raise £1350 by lottery for the rebuilding and further extension of the wharf and when the British evacuated the town in 1779 they burnt the wharf and its destruction as a commercial center was complete. In 1862 the trustees gave the railroad company a lease for 100 years at an annual rental of $1400, the company to keep it in good, sound and serviceable repair and thus the visitor will observe how well this condition is performed. The rents accruing have been used in the erection of two substantial school houses for this section of the city with the probability of another in the near future. Continuing our way and as we pass the boat shops we will stop and engage a boatman to meet us at the City Pier at the foot of Elm Street for a short sail after our walk up **Washington street**. We soon come to the old railroad depot and turning the corner are on Washington street, by the docks of the Old Colony Steamboat Company where may possibly be seen one or more of their huge floating palaces, by the boiler shop, and we are abreast of a spot that was but a few years ago used as a ship building establishment where were built many of the vessels that sailed from this port when its commercial interests were more prosperous than they are now. Passing by a large plain looking house with its glistening white exterior we come to the **Hunter house** on the left which was the residence of Dr. William Hunter who came from England in 1752 and was a renowned physician and surgeon and was the first practitioner in America to give a course of lectures on anatomy. It was while the British occupied the town that he contracted disease from a patient which caused his death, and it was here that Admiral de Ternay of the French force breathed his last, and this house is but one of the many houses of the city that has a varied history which tends to carry one back in imagination to the past glories of the place. We go by an opening leading to the water front with its long wooden pier and which is the City pier previously mentioned, passing by the house of Dr. H. R. Stover who also owns the Hunter house, while on the opposite side of the street are a colony of summer houses, we near the Cope house and that of Benjamin Smith while to our right on the opposite corner is the summer home of Mrs. Smith, by the row of poplar trees on either side with their arching branches interlocking, forming a bower over the street, by the house of Mrs. M. H. Sanford and Murray Shipley next beyond, with that of Edwin G. Angell across the way, and the next that of Jane Morris and Chas. Fairchild we come to a vacant lot opposite the stone house owned by Theo. A. Havemeyer we enter and follow the path leading to the shore and here we find the "**Blue Rocks**" a favorite resting place on a summer eve for a Romeo and Juliet, while in the lot adjoining are the ruins of the North Battery or as now known **Fort Greene** and originally was an earthwork thrown up during one night in 1776 and garrisoned by a detachment of soldiers with its guns trained on the British frigate Scarborough lying at anchor close to the shore and when morning dawned the vessel was obliged to beat a hasty retreat, it was finally completed as a harbor defense in 1798–1800 and named in honor of General Greene of Revolutionary fame. To the northward is seen the **Naval Training Station** of the U. S. Government. Across the bay is the new summer resort of Jamestown, and following the outline of the shore we obtain a fine view of the entrance to our Bay. Retracing our steps to the City Pier we embark in the sailboat previously engaged and sail up to the Training Station situated on an island known to the Indians in ancient times as " Weenat Shassit " which was afterwards changed by the settlers to Coasters Harbor Island. It is here that the future seamen of our Navy are educated in all that appertains to a first class man-of-war's man, and was established in 1881 by and through the active influence of Admiral Porter. Here the boys are instructed in an ordinary English education alternating with practical seamanship and other nautical operations, including many months of actual sea life on board of the several vessels belonging to this branch of naval service which yearly make long voyages to foreign shores. The applicant must be a native born American between the ages of 14 and 18 years and if accepted by the examining board after all preliminary requirements are completed the sailor boy's life begins on shore and in about six months he is transferred to one of the sea going ships and if proficient at the end of the voyage is drafted to the regular man-of-war where he finishes his term of enlistment or till he becomes of age. And in no sense is this branch of service a reformatory institution. Now heading across the Bay by the Gull Rocks with its wedge shaped lighthouse, by Rose Island with its old fort and crumbling barracks, built in the days of the Revolution as a harbor defence and known as Fort Hamilton and is owned by the government as a storage magazine of the dangerous explosives manufactured at the Torpedo Station and soon we approach the

shore of Conanicut Island whose surface is dotted with many summer residences, skirting its shore there soon opens up to view the
rocky headland known as the "**Dumplings**" on which is perched
a quaint, round ruin, built as a fort, and which has been a prominent
landmark to the entrance of our bay since the begining of the present century. Again sailing across the bay we pass the frowning walls
of Fort Adams, the second largest fortification in the United States,
by the wharf and into the harbor, passing the home of Ida Lewis
on the Lime Rocks, we sail by Goat Island, or better known as the
Torpedo Station, where the most destructive outfits of modern naval
warfare are constructed, and where our naval officers receive their
practical instruction in the manufacture and use of torpedoes and
high explosives. Passing between the many pleasure crafts at
anchor by the city wharf, we near the end of our marine excursion, and disembarking, wend oar way over Long Wharf to our
starting point, the Parade.

CHAPTER VIII.

E will now take a stroll down **Thames Street** and observe as we go along some of the historic buildings. **The City Hall** at our right, on the corner of Long Wharf, was erected in 1763 with funds raised by lottery, a custom much in vogue in olden times, and from plans drawn by Peter Harrison, a very prominent architect of his day. Its style is of the Ionic style of architecture, and was early known as the Brick Market or Granary. Its lower floor was open to the street and was occupied by market-men, and the upper story as a theatre, and was devoted to its present use in 1853. On the right and a little ways beyond is seen a wooden archway or passage leading down to the water front, and was known as the "**Arcade**," and in its day was quite a business place. In its immediate vicinity, a few doors below, is a building now occupied by the Boston Store, on whose front may be seen in carved letters the name **Wanton Building**, which was the home of one of Rhode Island's early governors, Gov. Joseph Wanton, who filled the office from 1769 until Nov. 7, 1775. Although the building has been modernized and enlarged, it still retains in its exterior some of its colonial features. As we go along

and come to the store of C. F. Frasch on our left, we look up the
courtway and observe the old **Sueton Grant House**, with its
second story overhanging the lower one, and with its massive stone
chimney with its encircling band of iron, a striking contrast to
the chimneys of the present day. This is one of three houses situated quite near to each other that were thus placed, as it was originally intended to have Thames street much wider than it is now,
and these houses marked the eastern boundary of the street line.
Still wending our way along the street we approach an iron fence
surmounting its stone base, and beyond stands the house that was

built and occupied by Jaheel Brenton as early as 1720, and later by
Walter Channing, two names prominent in Newport history, while
a little farther on will be seen on either side, just above the shop
doors, **Two Carved Eagles** surmounting a ball. These are the
ornaments which were once perched on the gate posts at "Vaucluse," mentioned in our trip out on the island. Originally they
were brought from England and came into the possession of a Mr.
Metcalf Bowles, who was occupying "Vaucluse" previous to the
Revolution, and later they were brought into this city were they
were placed, one on the Eagle Tavern and the other on the Engs

building, that on the Eagle Tavern, after passing through the hands of several owners, finally came into possession of Mr. Hammett, and who, fortunately for the history of the birds, occupies the building directly opposite the Engs estate. While down the wharf on our right may be seen a row of buildings painted a dark red, which were formerly used for various purposes by Aaron Lopez, one of Newport's early and successful Hebrew merchants, whose remains are quietly resting in the cemetery on the hill, of which Longfellow makes mention in one of his poems. Continuing on we come to Church street on the left, up which, a few steps on the right, will be seen a small two-story gambrel roofed house painted drab, with its doors on the street side cut horizontally, as was the custom in olden times; and this old building was known as the Assembly Rooms. Continuing our way a few blocks, and on our right we pass **Market Square**, on which is situated the police station, where but a few years ago was an old building known as the Market, and its business was conducted somewhat after the style of those in the South, only on a smaller scale. Continuing our way again we pass the **Free Library** on our left, the result of the generosity of our former citizen, Christopher Townsend, who bequeathed a large property, the income of which is used for its maintenance. Adjoining this building and situated on the corner of Pelham street, on which site was formerly the Eagle Tavern, and the present building, was the famous Townsend's Coffee House, and finally the United States Hotel. It is this place in the early colonial days that Fenimore Cooper refers to in his novel, the Red Rover, while on the opposite side of the street is Bannister's wharf, that leads to the harbor front, and was formerly the scene of great commercial activity. Passing along we come to a brick building on the left, occupied by two banks on the ground floor, while the rooms above are used by a club known as the **Business Men's Association**. We go by a few more of the older buildings of this street and approach the **Custom House and Post Office Building** at the corner of Franklin street, while in a niche of the building will be seen, guarded by a fancy grating, a bust of Benjamin Franklin, an early visitor to this town, and whose nephew, James Franklin, early started in the printing business, establishing the Newport Mercury in 1758, which paper has been published weekly (except during the occupancy of the town by the British) by its various proprietors up to the present time. It is here that we will board the street car and take a trip to the Mile Corner. We pass the Congregational Church on our right, and on the adjoining corner on the same side is the Sayer estate, which was occupied in 1776 by **General Prescott** as his headquarters in the town at the time he was in command of the British army, while on our left will be seen the old Trinity Church, with its varied history, of which we will make mention in another chapter. As our trip progresses we soon come to the First Baptist Church, the oldest Baptist Church in America, and on the next block, situated a few feet from the street, is the oldest house in the city, although somewhat modernized. It is known as the **Governor Bull House**, and was built in 1639 by Henry Bull, one of the early settlers, and who was governor of the State under the Royal Charter for one year from May, 1685, and also for a short period in 1690, and in 1912 it was a place of refuge from an attack of the Indians. We now pass from the narrow limits of Spring street and are on Broadway, while on the right will be seen a stone wall capped with an iron fence enclosing a fine piece of real estate belonging to Major Bull of the present day. A curious and interesting fact in connection with it is, that there is no deed to it nor record of any. It belonged to an ancestor of Major Bull, who was one of the eighteen original settlers who came to this island in 1638, when the island was first bought of the Indians, and in the division of the land Mr. Bull's portion extended from the old house just passed to Mann avenue, and the property has descended from father to son for over two centuries. Passing a few more of the colonial houses we soon approach the **Soldier's and Sailor's Monument**, dedicated May 23, 1899, to the memory of those brave men who gave up their lives in defence of their country in the war of the Rebellion, while beyond may be seen the **Calvert Schoolhouse**, named in honor of our late citizen, Hon. George H. Calvert, and is one of the many public institutions that Newporters are justly proud of. We are now going through the newer part of the city, by the residences of many of its successful merchants, and soon reach the terminus of the car route. Returning over the same route until Franklin street is reached, we extend our ride to the southern part of the city, and soon pass the **St. Mary's Church** (R. C.) on the left, with the convent opposite, while in the rear of the church may be seen a part of the massive stone schoolhouse and its brick rectory. We now cover quite a stretch of territory and soon pass the Emmanuel Church (P. E.) on the right and another one of the public schoolhouses on the left. **The Lenthal School**, named in honor of Robert Lenthal, "who, soon after the settlement of the island, was admitted a freeman by the General Court, and by a vote of the Town of Newport in 1640 was called to keep a public school for the education of youth, and for his encouragement, there were granted to him one hundred acres of land and four more acres for a house lot; and it was also voted one hundred acres more should be laid forth and appropriated for a school for the encouragement of the poorer sort to train up in learning; and Mr. Robert Lenthal, while he continues to teach school, is to have the benefit of said land," by the rear of some of the villas that front the avenue and we are soon at the southern terminus of the car route at Morton Park, Alighting from the car we enter the enclosure of the park and enjoy the scenery of the place. This park, containing twelve acres, was the gift of Vice President L. P. Morton to the citizens of Newport, and has been improved and its natural attractions made more attractive. Away to the south as far as the eye can reach is to be seen the broad Atlantic, while if we ascend the hill a view can be had of the harbor, while below us will be seen a large enclosure known as the Polo Grounds. It is here that society gathers several times each week during the summer to witness the games of polo, and at times it is quite exciting to watch the players riding their little ponies and rushing eagerly after the wooden ball, and with their mallets attempting to drive the ball over the line. It is on this hill during the progress of a game that the players have an enthusiastic audience, for to the citizens of Newport the spot is known as Dead-head Hill, where the best points of view may be had for nothing, while to gain entrance to the charmed circle of the enclosure one's purse strings have to be unloosened. Having had our fill of the beauty of this place we wend our way across the park again, board the car, and a few minutes' ride brings us to Franklin street, where we bid you adieu for a short time.

CHAPTER IX.

NOTHER enjoyable ride can be had on the island
by making our starting point from Touro Park to
Catherine street, which is the second street on our
right after passing **Redwood Library**, down which
we turn, going by some of the more aristocratic private boarding houses, and soon observe on our right a curious looking house, setting diagonally to the street, which is known as the
"Hypothenuse," and is the residence of Col. G. E. Waring, Jr.,
while next to him is the summer home of Miss Blatchford, with its
many little gables and open balconies, while in the next enclosure
is the villa of Mrs. Alexander Barret, and on the next corner is the
former home of the late Charlotte Cushman. Turning to our left
we enter upon **Rhode Island Avenue**, passing on the right the
elegant stone residence of A. C. Zabriski, surrounded with its granite wall, with that of Col. Addison Thomas adjoining, while the
second one beyond is that of L. Zabriski, and on the opposite side
of this pleasant street are the villas owned by Miss Woolsey, Miss
Yardley and Mrs. Noyes, while just beyond are the Hunter,
Stevens and Lieber villas, all very attractive houses for those de-
siring quietness and pleasant surroundings. Across the way on
the opposite corner on our left is the Sargent villa, and as we ride
along we go by many more homes occupied by our well-to-do merchants, who have selected this beautiful spot for their homes, away

from the bustling thoroughfare that has been entered into for business purposes. On our right we pass a strange looking building with its many projecting arms, giving it the appearance of some great marine monster; but be not alarmed, for it is here that the members of the St. George's Chapel meet for divine worship. Passing many more of the substantial looking residences and turning to the right we enter again into Broadway and pass along this road by the Mile Corner, until we come to the Two Mile Corner on our right where we will observe an old-fashioned guide board, which will direct us to the right down the **East, or Mail Road**, the latter name given it from the fact that previous to the entry of the steam cars to our city the only mode of travel by land was in the old-fashioned stage coach, which in those days transported the mail to and from Newport to Fall River and way places, and for years their route was over this road. Passing by the well tilled farms we soon approach **Slate Hill**, which, at its summit, is one of the highest points of land on the island, being about 200 feet above the sea level. Soon we open up to view on our right the South Portsmouth Post Office, while on the left but a short distance away is the **St. Mary's Church**, erected in 1844, through the generous endowment of Miss Sarah Gibbs, and who maintained it up to the time of her death in 1866. Since then it has been supported by voluntary contributions. The church property consists of about eighty acres, of which seven acres are devoted to the use of the rector, twelve acres are used for a free cemetery, while the balance is leased for farming purposes at a very low rental. After passing more of the well tilled farms we approach and pass on our left a historic place known as **Quaker Hill**, where in 1778, at the battle of Rhode Island, the British army was formed preparatory to the attempt to dislodge Gen. Greene, commanding the American forces. Still keeping to the right on this road until we reach Sprague lane, we make a detour around Butt's Hill on our left, another spot made prominent in the battle previously mentioned, for it was here that the British army held possession of the old fort, which still exists in its original form, giving a specimen of the engineering skill of a century ago. Alighting from the carriage we'll ascend the hill, where, from its summit, may be had a picturesque view that will repay the visitor. Entering our carriage again and resuming the drive, a few minutes' riding will bring us on the **West Road**, where we will have a fine view of the bay for quite a distance, by more of the fine farms, with here and there one of those quaint structures known as a Rhode Island windmill, where a particular kind of corn is ground into meal that is used in making the old-time famous "Johnny-cake," without which upon the table no breakfast was complete. In a short time we go over a bridge spanning a small stream which wends its way from another pleasant spot on the island lying beyond us and near the shore, known as "Lawton's Valley," by the **Redwood Farm** with its double row of lindens in front and its broad acres extending to the shore of the bay; that was in the long ago the country place of Abraham Redwood, of whom we speak more particularly in another chapter. A short distance beyond us we pass by Union street, down which a short distance is a charming little villa owned by Mrs. Julia Ward Howe. Still continuing along the West Road we soon approach and go by on our left a house said to have been the **Headquarters of General Prescott in 1775**. While the present structure occupies the site of the former house, there is but little of the earlier building in existence and that is an ell located in the rear, and it was at this spot that General Prescott was surprised and captured by that brave officer of the American army, Major William Barton, who, with his band of followers, safely eluded the eyes of the sentry on board of the British naval vessels anchored in the bay abreast of this place and safely passed the pickets stationed on the surrounding land, captured his prisoner, and without alarming the pickets, made his way by them and the several vessels and with his prisoner reached Providence in safety. The capture of this tyrannical officer was a source of great rejoicing to the inhabitants. We soon go by the grounds enclosed by a high wooden fence of the Aquidneck Agricultural Society on our right, and passing another of those old windmills come to Maple avenue on our right, down which we turn and go along the road skirting Coddington Point, by the residence of F. W. Andrews, of Boston, known as "Sunset Lawn," and soon come to Malbone Road, past "Malbone" and its beautiful surroundings, and soon are on Broadway again until we reach Cranston avenue on our right, through which we go to Kay street. Turning to the right, by Judge Gray's imposing villa known as "Hawshurst," by many other imposing villas surrounded by their large shade trees, and soon we come to the Jews' Cemetery on our left and the villa of G. M. Tooker opposite. Turning to the left again we are upon Bellevue avenue once more, along which we go until Touro Park is reached, where we will stop and bid you adieu.

CHAPTER X.

 S we have taken a number of drives and walks and seen most of the outlying parts of the city, we will visit a few of the historical places which will give us an inkling of what our sturdy ancestors went through and the benefits they enjoyed in the earlier days of the city's settlement. Let us visit **Trinity Church** and look at its quaint interior, with its high, old-fashioned pulpit and immense sounding board hung by a strong iron rod just over the preacher's head, looking more like a huge umbrella than anything else, while just beneath and in front of the pulpit is the little old desk where the clerk would assist the minister in conducting divine service in the long ago. Then again, notice the old square pews, wherein, in one, has sat George Washington, a name revered above all others by patriotic Americans, and from yon pulpit have preached such eminent divines as the Rev. James Honyman, Bishop Berkeley and Marmaduke Browne in the early days of the church. Dean Berkeley, afterwards known as Dr. George Berkeley, Lord Bishop of Cloyne, came to this country in 1728, remaining three years. He built the house known as Whitehall, situated in Middletown, and which we saw in our drive on the island, and he presented the church with a handsome organ in 1733, valued at £500, and the case still encloses the more modern interior. During the invasion of the

British in the Revolution the church was not desecrated by the
enemy, as were the other churches in the town, and to-day may be
seen a crown and two mitres on the organ, insignia of the British
authority, and cherished mementos of the days that tried the hearts
of men, while on the steeple above the vane is a perfect copy of the
British crown. After the evacuation of the town some young men
entered the church and despoiled it of the altar pieces, the King's
crown, lion and unicorn, and as evidence of their hatred of the invaders used it for a target. In 1725 the original church was built,
but owing to the increased number of worshippers the church was
enlarged to its present size, and to-day it is unable to accommodate
all who would attend divine service during the summer months.
The church has had many benefactors in its day, and as early as
1733 Nathaniel Kay, who was collector of customs, bequeathed his
house and ten acres of land to the church for the support of an as-
sistant minister, who was to act as schoolmaster in the education of
ten poor boys. In 1761 a part of the steeple was blown down during
a violent gale, and went through the roof of an adjacent house, and
three years later the steeple was struck by lightning and set on fire,
but was soon extinguished with little damage. On the walls may
be seen memorial tablets erected to the memories of Rev. Marmaduke
Browne and Salmon Wheaton, two of its former rectors; Oliver
Hazard Perry and several others. While in the silent graveyard lie
the remains of many of Newport's earlier inhabitants, all of whom
have worshipped in this edifice, where may be seen on the several
stones and monuments such names as Kay, Ayrault, Malbone,
James Honyman, Gidley, Hunter and Handy. Here may be seen
the monument erected to the memory of Chevalier de Ternay, who
was in command of the French navy which came to Newport during
the summer of 1780 to aid the colonists in their struggle for liberty
and co-operate with the Americans. He died here suddenly during
the winter of 1780 and was buried in these grounds, and later the
monument was erected by the King of France, and in 1874 the General Assembly of this State voted $800 to defray the expense of re-

pairing and protecting the same. Passing out into the street again a few steps along Spring street bring us to Mary street, down which we pass, and on the corner of the first street on our right will be seen the Vernon House. It is here that Count Rochambeau had his headquarters while the French army was in Newport, and it was to this place that General Washington was escorted after landing at Long Wharf and was received with such an ovation as only an American people can give to their deliverer from the bondage under which they had been placed by an enemy. Although the house has been modernized in its exterior it still retains its many colonial features inside, with its wide hallway extending from front to rear, its broad and massive stairway, its various rooms with their high panelled walls and all opening into the spacious hall. Here have been entertained many of the most prominent men of the olden time and where many fetes were held by the French officers, tendered to the fairest of the fair of Newport's daughters. Diagonally across the way is another remarkable specimen of colonial architecture known as the Chesbrough House. Passing through this street a short distance we come to the **Armory of the Newport Artillery**, the home of the oldest military organization in America, having been established in 1741. The present building was erected in 1836, and was enlarged a few years ago. As the armory is open for the inspection of visitors we enter its portals, where will be seen much of interest, among which may be mentioned a lock of hair of George Washington, as also of the Duke of Wellington, the hero of Waterloo. From the ranks of this company have been furnished men who have filled many important positions in the welfare of our country and our State, such names as Ward, Ellery and Marchant, members of the Continental Congress; Ellery, Malbone, Champlin and Hunter as Senators in Congress; Hazard, Pearce, Cranston and King as Representatives in Congress; while Ward, Lyndon and Gibbs as Governors of the State, as well as others who filled important offices in the French War of 1758 and the Revolutionary War of 1776. After looking the armory over we will pass along the street again towards the Mall, and turning to the right go up Touro street until we reach the **Jews' Synagogue**, built in 1762, the first house of worship erected by the Hebrews of America, while over the gateway of this enclosure may be seen the inscription : "Erected 5603, from a bequest made by Abraham Touro, Esq.," or in our notation of time 1842. The house is built in a substantial manner, while its interior is very plain, and forms a striking contrast with the more modern houses of worship of the present day. Divine worship is held here regularly during the summer months by Rabbi A. P. Mendes, for we have among us many of the Jewish faith. In the next enclosure we find the **Newport Historical Society**, occupying the building formerly belonging to the Seventh Day Baptists, and which building was erected in 1729, and is consequently the oldest building ever used as a meeting house in this city. We will enter the place, for the public are welcome. As we approach the steps, on the left of its doorway will be seen a little rounding window, which was the prevailing style of shop windows many years ago, and is the only one of its kind in existence in the place. Here will be seen the antiquities of Old Newport, the old pulpit and its quaint wooden sounding board projecting over it, while on either side of the pulpit will be seen two tablets bearing the Decalogue, the old Clagett clock still ticking away the flight of time as of yore, the old-fashioned spinning wheel, footstove and innumerable relics of bygone days. To the numismatist a sight is presented that will make the visit one of rare pleasure. To the horticulturist a sight will be seen to gladden the eye, for on the exterior of the building is a root of the ivy which was taken from Melrose Abbey and sent to Washington Irving by Sir Walter Raleigh, a gift to the society by one of its late members. We will not dwell longer on the sights of its rare curios, but will continue our stroll up the street a little further until we reach the cemetery on the hill, where lie interred the remains of many of Newport's former Hebrew inhabitants whose names have an important place in the history of the ancient town, such men as Touro, Reveira, Lopez and many others. Abraham

Touro, besides his gift to the synagogue, left a sum of money for the perpetual care and maintenance of the street bearing his name, and his brother Judah, who bequeathed a sum of money for the perpetual care of this graveyard, as also the sum of $10,000 to the city for the purchase of the piece of land for a park bearing his name, and which to-day keeps and probably forever will keep his name fresh in the minds of the citizen and visitor. Continuing along for a few steps we come to the **Redwood Library**, named in honor of Abraham Redwood, who was the founder and patron of the library. The society in 1747 obtained a charter from the colony by the name of "The Company of the Redwood Library." Mr. Redwood was ably assisted by Henry Collins, who presented to the company in 1748 the lot of land then known as "Bowling Green," on which the present building was erected. The building was completed in 1750 and has been enlarged several times since, and within its walls are rare books and works of art, as well as many relics of olden times, among which may be mentioned a jewel box made from a timber of the ship Endeavor, in which Captain Cook made his famous voyage around the world, a wooden pocket case, belonging to and used by Abraham Redwood, and a unique sideboard, which was originally the property of Nicholas Easton, one of the original settlers of the place. Still another memento of its founder is the iron gates on the north entrance to the enclosure, which once stood in front of the house occupied by Redwood on Thames street. The visitor while at this place should not fail to notice the massive tree, the **Fern Leaf Beech**, on the corner of the lot where Redwood street meets the avenue, which is a source of great pride not only to the Library Company but to the citizens as well. This tree was introduced here about 1840 by a wealthy Scotch gentleman named Johnstone, who was a resident of the place. When first planted it was about four feet high. Apropos of this may be mentioned a story of a man who had summered here, and who, having bathed in the waters of its many beaches, made diligent inquiry as to the location of the Fern Leaf Beech (beach) that he might bathe in it, and say on his departure that he had bathed in every beach hereabout. Leaving the library we stroll along the avenue and approach **Touro Park,**

where will be seen the famous " Round Tower," or perhaps better known as the " **Old Stone Mill,**" which is mentioned by the Poet Longfellow in his poem, " The Skeleton in Armor," in which the closing scene is laid

> " In that lofty tower,
> Which to this very hour
> Stands looking seaward."

The origin of this structure is mere conjecture. Some say it was built by the Norsemen who visited these shores before Columbus discovered America, others that it was the work of the early settlers and was used by them as a mill for grinding corn, while another claims that it was built as a place of refuge from the attacks of Indians, while Benedict Arnold, who once lived a short distance to the westward, speaks of it in his will as " my stone built windmill." Let these theories remain, as one is as correct as the other. In 1756 a lookout was built on top of the old structure, which then belonged to John Bannister. Tradition has it that the old structure is the abode of witches' souls and at the witching hour of midnight, under proper conditions, a person in love by walking around the mill seven times slowly, repeating at the same time certain cabalistic phrases, that the witches will appear to the romantic wooer. Be that as it may, so runs the tale. A short distance beyond and near the avenue stands the statue erected to the memory of **Commodore Matthew Calbraith Perry** (brother of Commodore O. H. Perry, whose statue was observed at the foot of the Mall), through the generosity of the late August Belmont, who married a daughter of Commodore Perry. The statue was designed by the sculptor J. Q. A. Ward and its pedestal by R. M. Hunt. On the upper belt is cut "Africa, 1843;" "Mexico, 1846;" "Treaty with Japan, 1854;" while under these, surrounding the circle, are bas-reliefs illustrating his services in those countries. On the lower belt is cut "Commodore Matthew C. Perry, U. S. N. Died 1858, aged 64." On the front of the plinth of the pedestal is cut an American eagle. On the north and south sides, an anchor, and in the rear, "Erected in 1868 by August Belmont and Caroline S. Belmont." The statue was dedicated with great honor, October 1, 1868. Still another object of historical interest, though situated in the north part of the city at the junction of Thames and Farewell streets, is the "Liberty Tree," so called. The original tree was a buttonwood tree erected by the "Sons of Liberty" to commemorate the act of rebellion against the infamous act of the British Parliament in passing the "Stamp Act" of 1776, and was cut down by the British when they occupied the town. In 1783 a second tree, a sycamore was planted. After it had attained its full growth, some thirty-seven years afterwards, the survivors of the "Sons" referred to placed upon it a large copper plate, upon which the names of those who planted it were engraved. The tree perished from disease about the year 1850 and was cut down. The copper plate, we believe, is in the possession of the Historical Society. In 1870 a third tree was planted, and is to-day enclosed by four granite posts and an iron fence, and is somewhat inappropriate to the spirit which prompted the planting of the first tree, an English oak as a symbol of American liberty.

A short distance from this spot and fronting on Thames street is another old landmark, the house wherein lived **William Ellery,** one of the signers of the Declaration of Independence, and whose descendants still occupy it. Continuing up Farewell street a few steps to the Cemetery we enter and pass through the grounds to the adjoining enclosure where will be seen a monument erected by the State of Rhode Island to commemorate the valor of Commodore Oliver Hazard Perry and beyond, in the upper part of the cemetery, will be seen the beautiful stone structure of the **Belmont Memorial Chapel,** erected by the generous hand of the late August Belmont (whose family plot fronts the chapel), and where the last sad rites may be conducted for the rich or poor of whatever religious belief "without money and without price." Passing out from this silent city of the dead we enter again into Farewell street and continue through, and by the North Baptist Church, facing which, across the narrow street, will be seen the **Coddington Burial Ground,** wherein lie the remains of several of Newport's original settlers. A wide headstone will be seen bearing this inscription : "This monument erected by the Town of Newport on the 12th day of May, 1830, being the second Centennial Anniversary of the settlement of this town, to the memory of William Coddington, Esq., that illustrious man, who first purchased the island from the Narragansett Sachems, Canonicus and Miantonomi, for, and on account of himself and seventeen others, his associates in the purchase and settlement. He presided many years as chief magistrate of the island and Colony of Rhode Island, and died much respected and lamented on the 1st day of November, 1678, aged 78 years, and was here interred." Here also is the monument to the memory of Governor Bull, on the north side of which is the following, viz.: "He was one of the eighteen original purchasers of this island who settled the town of Pocasset or Portsmouth in 1638, and one of eight who settled the town of Newport in 1639." On the east side : "Here lyeth interred ye body of Henry Bull, Esq., late Governor of this colony, aged 85 years, deceased Jan. ye 22, 1693-4 ;" and on the south side: "Elizabeth, his wife, died Oct. 1, 1665." "Anne Clayton, his second wife and widow of Nicholas Easton, died Jan. 30, 1707." Thus the visitor will see that we still have with us the reminders of the past bearing testimony to what occurred more than two and a half centuries ago. Continuing along the street we soon will see on the left, partly hidden by the trees and some distance back from the street, the meeting house of the Society of Friends, which was early established in this town and where they come annually for their meetings with members from different parts of the United States, and whose presence draws large audiences to listen to the remarks and learn of their simplicity of ways, and even this is rapidly giving away to more modern ideas of religious worship. A few steps more and we approach the old State House where we will leave you for the present.

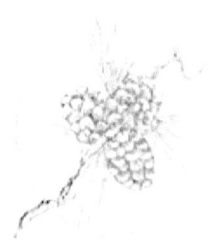

CHAPTER XI.

NOTHER place well worth observing is an island situated about half a mile from the wharves of the inner harbor, and known at the present time as the **Torpedo Station.** Its geographical name is Goat Island. Its shape is semi-elliptical and separates the inner from the outer harbor, and contains about seventeen acres. In 1657 the island was purchased by Benedict Arnold and John Greene from the Indians. As early as 1702 the first fort was built and called Fort Anne. A quarter of a century later another fort was erected and named Fort George. It was built and furnished with guns at the expense of the colony. In 1755 the General Assembly ordered the enlarging and rebuilding of the fort and voted £10,000 (old tenor), on condition that the town of Newport contributed £5,000 pounds. From the outbreak of the Revolution and until 1784 it was known as Fort Liberty, after which it was named Fort Washington, and early in the present century its name was again changed to Fort Wolcott, by which name it has been known until within a few years. At the breaking out of the War of the Rebellion the Naval Academy was removed here from Annapolis, Md., and was situated here until the close of the war. From that time until 1869, when the government established the Torpedo Station, it was the resort of many gay picnic parties during the summer months, and was quite an attractive place, the old fort and its crumbling walls and underground passages and its keeper, Sergeant Morrison, who has that fine military bearing like a soldier of the Continental army, and who was a pensioner of the war of 1812, and resided in the only building on the island, known as the barracks. Since the establishment of the Torpedo Station the island has un-

dergone great improvement, and where previously there was no other
building than the old barrack, to-day it has its many brick buildings
for the manufacture of torpedoes, guncotton and other explosives,
as also many cosy houses wherein reside the officers who are stationed here. Almost every year a class is appointed by the government for instruction, and is known as the torpedo class, consisting
of a score or more of naval officers whose duties while stationed here
are first in experimenting, then in the manufacture not only of the
various explosives but of the making of the various parts which go
to make up a complete torpedo outfit, and finally instruction. The
duties of the class begin in May and continue for three months, and
their labors are of the most exacting kind, combining severe work
and study. While to the visitor this may seem a pleasant part of
the duties connected with the naval service, to those engaged in the
work it is one of great effort and is connected with considerable risk,
as one false movement would probably entail the loss of life. But
such results are of rare occurrence, as the instructor and experi-
menter are very cautious in all their movements. There are several
high speed boats attached to the station, built by the Herreshoffs, of
Bristol, notably the "Lightning," which has made a speed of over
twenty miles an hour, and whose performance has not yet been
equalled by any craft of her size. Then there is the "Stiletto,"
whose speed has been remarkable. All the new inventions of torpedoes are given a most thorough trial at this station before adop-
tion into the naval service. Could the tourist visit the island much
would be seen of an interesting nature, but as the place is not open
to visitors we must content ourselves with a distant view. But
before leaving the city we must make a visit to **Fort Adams**, which
is best done by starting from Bannister's Wharf, where will be
found many safe and commodious sailboats in charge of skilful
boatmen, who will take us across the harbor in a few minutes, landing us at the wharf, where we will disembark and wend our way
along the road, past the sentry, through the sally-port into the enclosure. The original fort was built during the latter part of the

eighteenth century and was christened on the twenty-third anniversary of American independence with great pomp and military display and named Fort Adams, in honor of John Adams, who was President of the United States. The war of 1812 demonstrated the weakness of the fort, and after peace was declared the attention of Congress was called to the defenceless condition of the various fortifications, and a liberal appropriation was made for the reconstruction and enlargement of this fort, and on the 11th of May, 1825, the first stone of the new fort was laid, and after the lapse of many years it was completed and garrisoned in 1841. At the present time there are stationed here several companies of infantry and the light battery, together with a fine military band. As a general custom during the summer months there are various military drills carried on, which the public are allowed to witness, including guard mount and dress parade several mornings of each week, battalion drill twice, and inspection and dress parade once each week, as also a band concert twice each week, and to this last attraction the driveway of the parade grounds are well filled with carriages and their occupants, who come to listen to the music of the Fort Band. Having looked the place over and seen the various implements of warfare, ancient and modern, passed through some of the many underground passages, looked into the dark and dreary dungeons, we will wend our way to the boat again, embark, and after a short sail around the harbor or elsewhere as fancy may suggest, return to our starting point, Bannister's Wharf.

CHAPTER XII.

NOTHER pleasant trip can be taken to **Jamestown** or, as is often called, Conanicut, by going to Ferry Wharf or Market Square, for by both names is it known. Instead of the old-time custom of the boatman crying "Away! way! way!" to announce to the traveler that the ferry boat was about to start on its journey across the Bay,—the duration of the trip depended upon the force of the wind,—often taking an hour or more, we have now the staunch and commodious steam ferry boat "Conanicut" to take us across in twenty minutes. Hastening on board we soon hear a short blast of the whistle followed immediately by a stroke of the bell in the engine room and our trip begins. Out into the harbor, by Long Wharf and around the breakwater, extending several hundred feet from Goat Island, we soon pass Rose Island and in a few minutes approach the landing at Jamestown. Engaging one of the many conveyances to be found at the landing we will take a drive about the island and notice the many pretty cottages to be found there.

Jamestown was incorporated as a town November 4, 1678, and was named in honor of King James II., and the island was, while the Indians possessed it, known as "Quononoqutt," which soon became Conanicut. In 1885 its population was 516. As the inhabitants are constantly changing, only twice since the last census has it had more than this number of inhabitants, and that of 1755 and 1774, when it numbered 517 and 563 respectively, while the last census of 1890 gave it a population of 707. That the people were slow to improve each shining hour goes without saying. As far back as 1725 the General Assembly was petitioned by residents of Newport for the right to establish a ferry between Jamestown and Newport, which was granted, and the old-time ferryboat was run until 1872, when the present company was organized and built a steam ferryboat to take the place of the old-timer. This was a great innovation for the more conservative citizens, but it was the beginning of a new era. A larger and faster boat was required, and with the quicker means of passing between Newport and Jamestown persons travelled to the island oftener. Capitalists invested in the lands, platted the property and placed in on the market. It was but a little while before a house lot was sold and then another, and the land began to rise in value. Boarding houses were opened, people were attracted to the place on account of its quietness and nearness to gay Newport. Soon the boom in real estate began and has continued ever since, and to-day can be seen hundreds of houses that are owned and occupied by people from New York, Philadelphia, Baltimore and other cities. Where a few years ago there were a few boarders taken by the farmers, to-day shows several large hotels with their many hundreds of summer guests. In fact so much excitement has been caused that one person who owned a lot of land here and a large house on the Island of Rhode Island, caused it to be moved across the bay on scows and placed on its foundation on this island, and is the only house on the island that was thus transported, although there exists a house at this place that once was situated in Tiverton, but it was carefully taken to pieces, the lumber brought here and the house rebuilt.

There are several places of historic interest on the island which we will notice in their proper place. The first point of interest that we will visit lies to the south end of the island and is known as **Beaver Tail Lighthouse**, which is best reached by taking the road across the island, by the hotels, churches and post-office, until we approach a church on our right, when we turn to the left on to the road known as Southwest avenue, over which we go and across the narrow neck of land separating the water of Sheffield pond on our right from that of Mackerel cove on our left while the beach to the left is known as Partridge beach. Our ride now takes us over the rugged road through several farms and swampy places, and soon we reach our destination, Beaver Tail. Here will be had a fine view of the mighty ocean;—on our right can be seen the frowning cliffs known as **The Bonnet**, and where on the morning of Nov. 6, 1880, during a dense fog, the palatial steamer Rhode Island with her living cargo of about 200 souls went ashore and afterwards became a total loss, but fortunately no lives were lost. A short distance beyond this place and to the southward will be seen a lonely light-house situated on what is known as "**Whale Rock**," and a very dangerous locality it is for the mariner, as the rocks are only in sight at low water, and many a fine vessel has met her fate at this place previous to, as well as since the erection of this lighthouse, while still farther away may be seen that gay resort of Narragansett Pier, a harmless rival of Newport.

A short distance in front of us and beyond the white capped breakers will be seen a black can buoy marking **Newton Rock** and warning the mariner to pass it at a safe distance. To our left will be seen the shores of Rhode Island and Brenton's Reef light-ship beyond. Let us visit the lighthouse whose keeper is that genial host, Captain Wales, who will explain the various duties connected with its care and maintenance and also show the visitor the working of the steam siren whose doleful sound can be heard for miles around and perhaps for days at a time during our foggy season. At this spot in 1730 was erected the first lighthouse on our coast, being built of wood, by order of the General Assembly. It was destroyed by fire in 1753 and the Assembly immediately ordered a new one to be constructed of brick and stone, which after doing service for many years was destroyed by the British on the day of the evacuation in 1779, and was subsequently rebuilt, since which time it has continued without interruption to shed its guiding rays upon all who by night have sailed in or out of the Bay.

Returning over the same roadway until we come to Partridge Beach again, we follow the road skirting Mackerel Cove, and soon pass the residence of Joseph Wharton, situated on Southwest Point, and soon approach and pass the villa of W. T. Richards, the famous artist, and still following the winding road, with the ocean in view, we soon pass the residence of C. W. Wharton, situated on High Hill and but a short distance from the old ruins known as "**Fort Dumpling**," which we will inspect. This fort was built during the administration of President John Adams, 1797-1801, and has been

known at various times as Fort Louis, Fort Brown, but for the greater part of the time since its construction it has been known as Fort Dumpling. It was never garrisoned and has been allowed to decay, and before the boom of Jamestown as a summer resort was the favorite stamping ground of picnic parties and the campers-out. It is situated on a high headland, and from its walls a very fine view can be had of the entrance to our beautiful bay, with the frowning walls of Fort Adams across the bay and Castle Hill beyond. While on the shore side we can see the lighthouse that we just visited, and stretching away in the distance can be seen **Point Judith**, and with certain conditions of the atmosphere Block Island may be seen. Re-

suming our drive we pass in sight of the cottage of Commodore Self-
ridge perched upon its rocky height, and a short distance beyond is
an unique villa owned by D. S. Newhall, of Philadelphia, which is
known as the "Ship," but without any characteristics of a vessel,
unless it is that it resembles somewhat the turret of some abandoned
monitor. We pass many more of the pretty cottages situated in
the immediate vicinity, and soon come to the road which passes
across the island from the East to the West Ferry, on to which we
will turn and drive to the West Ferry, where during the summer
months the old ferryboat Jamestown, which formerly ran to Newport, is employed to carry passengers across the West Bay to
Eaton's Ferry on the Narragansett shore, where also a ride can be
continued some seven miles through the country to Narragansett
Pier.

A short distance from the ferry landing is an island known as
Dutch Island, which forms the outer boundary of a harbor of the same
name, which is a safe anchorage for hundreds of vessels during a
storm. On the island are the remains of many buildings that were
occupied by the workmen employed in constructing a battery that
was built there by the government. The island was used during
our late war as a camp for the colored troops previous to their departure for the front, and the only occupants of the island at the
present time is an ordnance sergeant, who is in charge of the government property, and his family. There is no historical interest
connected with it other than that mentioned. Returning we come to
the church on the corner of the main road, turning to the left we
pass on to this road and will continue our drive over this almost
straight road to the northern end of the island and to another summer colony known as "**Conanicut Park**," which was the first place
selected for a summer home on the island, prior to the boom of
Jamestown. Going over several bridges spanning the creek and
pond, by many well tilled farms, through the wild woodland known
as "**Lover's Lane**," and soon we approach the outskirts of the Park
and here, partly hidden by the trees surrounding it, is the oldest

house on the island formerly known as the **Capt. Kidd House** and where this bold buccaneer was wont to stop when on the island. The house was originally built over two hundred years ago, but since the present owner bought it it has been modernized to such an extent that many of its old features are lost sight of. Another historic house is what is now known as Seaside Cottage, owned by a religious society of Providence, and formerly known as the **Hopkin House** where once lived Stephen Hopkins, a signer of the Declaration of Independence.

Continuing our drives through the various avenues of Conanicut Park by the pleasant homes of its sojourners we see much to please the eye and cause us to desire that we were one of the favored ones to pass a pleasant summer at this quiet retreat and within short distance and easy access to the bustling city. Conanicut Park comprises a large part of the north end of the island with an area of something like five hundred acres, and is owned by a corporation under a charter granted in 1873 by the General Assembly. The place has its hotel and church and its summer population is several hundred. But we must return to Jamestown, and passing over the only road existing between the north and south end of the island we soon reach the end of the drive and turning to the left go along to the water front and thence to our starting point. Boarding the steam ferry boat a few minutes sail brings us to Newport again where we bid you adieu for the season of 1891.

SUMMER RESIDENTS.

C Signifies, Occupied by Owner.

Name	City	Villa/Cottage	Location	Owner
Acosta, Mrs	Baltimore		Shepard av	
Agassiz, Prof Alex	Cambridge		Castle Hill	
Agassiz, Max	Cambridge		Castle Hill	
Almou, Andrew D	Salem		Red Cross ave	
Amory, Howard C A	New York	Bateman's	Bateman's Point	
Amory, J H	New York	Bateman's	Bateman's Point	
Andrews, Frank W	Boston	Sunset Lawn	Maple ave, Coddington Pt	
Andrews, Paul	Boston	Sunset Lawn	Maple ave, Coddington Pt	
Arnold, Olney 2nd	Providence		71 Washington st	E G Angell
Arnold, Dr E S F	Yonkers	Hawthorne Villa	Carroll & Bateman aves	
Astor, William	New York	Beechwood	Bellevue ave & Cliffs	
Aucirlachus, Mrs F	New York		184 Washington st	
Auchincloss, John W	New York	Hammersmith Farm	Harrison ave	
Auchincloss, Henry B	New York		181 Washington st	
Austin, William	New York		Ocean House	
Bailey, C H	Philadelphia	Maitland Cottage	Cypress st, end of 51st	
Bailey, H	Philadelphia	Maitland Cottage	Cypress st, end of 2 st	
Bailey, S H	Philadelphia	Maitland Cottage	Cypress st, end of 51st	
Baker, Mrs Richard	Boston		Bellevue ave & Ledoe road	
Baldwin, Charles A	New York		Casino Club	
Baldwin, C C	New York	Chateau Nooga	Bellevue av & Narragansett av	
Baldwin, M s Chas H	New York	Sand Harbor	Bellevue av & Ruggles av	
Baldwin, Miss	Philadelphia		Ocean House	
Barclay, George	Washington D C	Cozy Cottage	33 Bath Road	
Barger, Samuel F	New York		Bellevue ave & Perry st	
Barret, Mrs Alexander	New York	Fair Haven	61 Catherine st	
Barstow, Miss K R	Boston		East stone	
Beach, Mrs C N	Hartford	Hegresse	Kay & Ayrault st	
Bigelow, Henry	New York	Malzone	Malzone road	
Beekman, James H	New York	Mayeroft	428 Bellevue ave	Pomeroy
Bell, Dr C M	New York		Bellevue av Lake View av	
Bell, Isaac	New York	Davis Chalet	Cliffs & Bailey's Beach	Est A Smith
Belmont, Mrs August	New York	By-the-Sea	Bellevue ave & Cliffs	
Belmont, O H P	New York	By-the-Sea	Bethville ave & Cliffs	
Belmont, Perry	New York	By-the-Sea	Bellevue ave & Cliffs	
Bentley, George	Germantown, Pa		Ocean House	
Bentley, Henry	Germantown, Pa		Ocean House	
Beresford J G	New York	Beach Rock	Harrison ave	E D Morgan
Berryman, C H	New York	Dolwin	261 Gibbs ave	O H Burgess
Berwind, E J	New York	The Elms	Bellevue ave & Dixon st	
Best, Col C L	New York		Bellevue ave & Perry st	
Bininger, W B	New York		Ocean House	
Binney, Horace			Western Cottage	
			64 Ayrault st	Mrs Admiral Reed Worden
Binney, William	Providence		84 Catherine st	
Bishop, Robert R	New York	Lofredre Villa	Ochre Point & Ruggles ave	Mrs J H Eldridge
Bishop Henry R	New York	O'Donnell Villa	Ochre Point ave	Miss O'Donnell
Batchelor, Judge Samuel	Washington D C		28 Greenough Place	
Blatchford, Mrs R H		Newman Cottage	24 Catherine st	Miss Newman
Blatchford, Miss S E	New York		87 Catherine st	
Blewitt, Albertson	Philadelphia	Shady Nook	Bellevue ave, n Webster st	
Boshhaver H W	New York	Wynnwyn	Paradisy road	
Booth, Edwin	New York	Boothden	Indian ave	
Borden, Jerome C	Fall River	House No 2	Ocean ave	
Bofden, Theo o	Fall River	Goose Neck	Ochre ave	
Boyd, Mrs Marta	Philadelphia	Liebe Cottage	Rhode Island ave	Mrs Lider
Brackett, W H	Chicago		Ocean ave	
Brewster, Mrs C B	Boston	Torm and Cottage	Kay & Ayrault st	Mrs C Townsend
Branko, H Mortimer	New York	Rockhurst	Bellevue ave & Cliffs	
Brown, Edward S	New York	Cram Villa	Near Second Beach	Cram
Brown, Mrs J C	Providence		Bellevue & Hazard ave	
Brown, Harol l	Providence		Bellevue & Hazard ave	
Brown, John Nicholas	Providence		Bellevue, opp Leroy ave	
Bryen, Mrs Mary A D	Boston	Ilion Villa	40 Bellevue ave	
Bryce J Smith	New York		46 Bellevue ave	
Bryce, Carroll	New York		Near Ochre side corner	
Bull, Charles M	Brooklyn		Bellevue & Ruggles ave	
Burden, I Townsend	New York	Fairlawn	Sunnyside	Mrs C P Clackering
Burden William F	Troy, N Y		Bellevue ave	
Burnett, Mrs M A	New York	Shields Villa	Ruggles ave	C W Shields
Butts, George W, Jr	Providence	Chanler Villa	Cliff View ave	Chanler
Caldwell, The Misses	New York		48 Kay st	
Caswell, John R	New York		21 Bull st	
Chandler, A E	Montreal		Ocean House	
Chapman, J F	New York		101 Washington st	T A Havemeyer
Clark, Mrs M A	East Boston	Maitland Cottage	Cypress, end of Second st	
Clevea of Dr Clement	New York		21 Merton road	
Clews, Henry	New York	The Rocks	Ocean ave	
Clyne, J L	New York		Parker ave	
Colman, Mrs M P R	Boston		Ocean House	
Codman, Ogden, Jr	Boston	The Berkeley	Jones st and Bellevue ave	Mrs M A C Holmes
Coffin, F N	Chicago		Bellevue & Narragansett av	
Coles, Mrs Elizabeth	New York	Verlbee	81 Bellevue ave	
Colford, Sidney Jones	New York	Conkling Cottage	Touro Park, west	A R Conkling
Comfort, Howard	Germantown	Maitland Cottage	Cypress st, end of Second	
Cook, Henry H	New York	Sea Verge	Bellevue ave and Cliffs	
Cook, Mrs Joseph I	Providence		Near Ochre side corner	
Cook, Prof Joseph P	Cambridge		Gibbs ave and Buena Vista	
Cope, Marmaduke C	Philadelphia		67 Washington st	
Colt, Mrs T H W	Bristol		Ocean House	
Cowley, T S	Montreal		Ocean House	
Cram, Henry A	New York	Snuds' Villa	Le Roy Road	Est Mahlon Sands
Crisser Mrs Blanche	New York	Terry Cottage	Gibbs ave	Res Roderick Terry
Cullum, Gen Geo A	New York		Sea View ave	
Cunningham, Dr E L	Boston		Catherine and Cottage sts	
Cushing, Thomas F	Boston	New Ladee	Bellevue ave and Cliffs	
Cutting, Robert L	New York		Ocean House	
Cutting, F B	New York	Palmer Cottage	Bellevue ave	Miss Ogden
Cutting Mrs Brockholst	New York	Palmer Cottage	Bellevue ave	Miss Ogden
Cutting, William, Jr	New York	Palmer Cottage	Bellevue ave	Miss Ogden
Dardenville Jules	New York		51 Everett Place	J P Vernon
Derby, J F	Philadelphia		Ocean House	
Davenport Mrs H	New York		2 Merton Road	
Davis, Julien F	New York	Finecroft	Purgatory Road	
Davis M s Anna W	Philadelphia		61 Washington st	T A Havemeyer

Name	City	Residence	Address	Owner/Agent
Davis, Ellwood	Philadelphia	Hodges	52 Catherine st	
Davis, Theodore M	New York		Ocean ave	
DeForest, George B	New York	Train Villa	Bellevue ave & Cliffs	Heirs of A Smith
Delton, Mrs Theodore	New York	Acosta Villa	Shepard & ochre Point av	Mrs. M. C. Acostor
DeMessimey, Vincent	New York	The Berkeley	John st & Bellevue ave	
DePeyster, The Misses	New York		Chandler st & Redwood ave	C. Mason
Dickey, The Misses	New York	Creighton Cottage	Bay st	J. McF. Creighton
Dilloway, W. E.	Boston	Airlie Louise	Bellevue ave	Mrs. B. W. Tennant
Dore, Mrs Engeline	New York	Dahlen	20 Gibbs ave	O. H. Burrows
Dresser, The Misses	New York		36 Bellevue ave	Mrs. H LeRoy
Duncan, George	Boston	Cushman Villa	R I ave & Catherine st	N. C. Cushman
Duncan, W R	Boston	Cushman Villa	R I ave & Catherine st	F. C. Cushman
Duncan, W R Jr	New York		Casino Club	
Earl, William D	Nashua		29 Merton Road	
Early, Charles	Washington		Ocean House	
Edgar, Mrs William	New York	Hollywood House	2 Bench st	
Exeler, Hubert	Jersey City	Maitland Cottage	Cypress st end of Second st	
Elliot, John	Boston	Howe Cottage	Lawton's Valley	Mrs. J. W. Howe
Elliot, Richard	Philadelphia	Wheeler Cottage	Coddington ave	Mrs. Chas. Wheeler
Ellis, John W	New York	Stoneacre	Bellevue & Victoria ave	
Emmons, Arthur B	Boston		14 Gibbs ave	
Erving, Mrs Shirley	Boston	Terrell House	Kay and Bull st	J. N A Griswold
Fairchild, Chas F	Boston		84 Washington st	
Farrberton, H. P	Croton on the Hds'n		Ocean House	
Fearing, Daniel B	Newport		84 Ashland de road	
Fearing, George R	New York	The Orchard	314 Narragansett ave	
Fearn, Walker	Chicago	Dess Villa	Easton's Point	Mrs. Z. C. Dess
Ferhan, Archbishop	Chicago		Ocean House	
Ferban Miss	Chicago		Ocean House	
Fish, Stuyvesant	New York	Peterson Villa	Balts road	Mrs. O J Peterson
Fiske, Josiah M	New York	Masoulea	Rough's ave & Cliffs	
Floyd, G W	Revere, Mass	Maitland Cottage	Cypress st end of Second st	
Ford, Mrs A	Boston	Maitland Cottage	Cypress st end of Second st	
Ford, A Jr	East Boston	Maitland Cottage	Cypress st end of Second st	
Foster, John	Boston	Ridge Lawn	LeRoy av	
Fowler, Charles E	New York		Ocean House	
Francis, Rev Lewis	Brooklyn	Witherbee Cottage	Honyman Hill	S H Witherbee
Freeman, Francis P	New York	Tower Top	Bellevue & Victoria ave	
French, Francis O	New York	Harbor View	Chartellows ave	
French, Seth Barton	New York	Cliff Lawn	Cliffs	Chanler Est
Fry, Gen James B	New York	Malcom Cottage	58 Kay st	Rev. C H Malcom
Gammell, R. H. I	Providence	Ocean Lawn	Narragansett av and Cliffs	
Gammell, Mrs William	Providence	Ocean Lawn	Narragansett av and Cliffs	
Gardner, Mrs	Philadelphia	Hodeca	52 Catherine st	
Garrett, Mrs G L	New York	Conkling Villa	Touro Park, west	A B. Conkling
Gibbes, Miss Emily O	New York	Mabelubn	87 Gibbs ave	
Gibbes, Miss Sarah B	New York		Buena Vista st and R. I. av	
Gibbs, Major Theo K	New York	Bethabn	Gibbs ave	
Giddes, Professor Walcott	Cambridge		Bellevue ave	
Gilbert, Mrs J T	New York		Bellevue ave	
Gibson, J. H	Philadelphia	Maitland Cottage	Cypress st end of Second	
Gillget, Horatio	Milton, Mass	Bateman's	Bateman's Point	
Godbold C	Chelsea, Mass	Maitland Cottage	Cypress st end of Second	
Goelet, Ogden	New York	Kingscote	Bellevue opp Ocean House	D. King
Goelet, Robert	New York		Narragansett av and Cliffs	
Gray, Judge John O	New York	Hawkhurst	Kay st and Cranston ave	
Gray, John A C	New York	Finigelly Villa	Gibbons near Catherine st	
Green, Mrs J C	New York	Pinard Cottage No 4	Narragansett ave	C. & J A Pinard
Green, William Brenton	New York		Malbone road & Broadway	
Griswold, J N A	New York	Seawold	Ocean avenue	
Grosvenor, William	Providence		Beacon Hill	
Grosvenor, Miss	Providence		Beacon Hill	
Hall, Lt Martin E , U. S. N.		Pell Cottage	Greenough Place	
Hardens, Miss Sallie	New York	Train Villa	Bellevue ave	Heirs of A Smith
Harriman, J Low	New York	Eldredge Villa	Ochre Pt and Ruggles av	Mrs. J H Eldredge
Havemeyer, Theo A	New York	Freidham	Bellevue & Coggeshall ave	
Hayden, Dr D H	New York		Red Cross & Buena Vista sts	
Hazard, R N	New York	Finehyrst	One mile corner	
Herrick, E J	New York	Daisy Bank	Clay st and Park r ave	
Hill G H H	New York	Hoffman Villa	Bellevue ave and Cliffs	Miss S.O. Hoffman
Hitchcock, Mrs Thomas	New York	Gravel Court	Clay st & Narragansett av	Mrs Geo Tiffany
Hitchcock, Center	New York	Gravel Court	Clay st & Narragansett av	
Hodgson, J M	New York		LeRoy ave	
Holmes, Mrs Mary A C	Boston	Rockoy Hall	Narragansett & Bellevue av	
Home, Robert S	New York	Wee Holm	Spring st	
Horton, S M	Newport		95 Pelia st	
Hotchkiss, Mrs M E	New York		Ocean House	
Howard, Mrs F W	New York		22 Kay st	
Howe, Mrs Julia Ward	Boston		Lawton's Valley	
Howe, Mrs Walter	New York		Bevan Hill road	
Hoyt, Henry S	New York	Inglewood	31 Bench st	
Hoyt, Winfield S	New York		Casino Club	
Hunt, R M	New York	Hill Top Cottage	9 Bellevue ave	
Hunt, Jane	New York		88 Ayrault st	
Huntington, Samuel	Brooklyn	Broadlawn	Ridge road, Castle Hill	
Hutton, G M	Baltimore	Shamrock Cliff	Ridge road, Castle Hill	
Hyde, Mr	Plainfield, N. J		Ocean House	
Isermood, Mrs Sarah E	Philadelphia	Reef Point	Yznaes ave & Cliffs	
Jackson, Mrs F W	New York	Zabriskie Villa	Rhode Island ave	
Jay, Col. William	New York	Cottage X	Easton's Beach	Land Trust Co
Johnson, H A	New York	Eustis Villa	Gibbs ave	Mrs. M. C. Eustis
James, Miss C Ogden	New York		Ruggles ave & Cliffs	
Jones, Mrs George F	New York	Pen Craig	Harrison ave	
Jones, Harry E	New York	Pen Craig	Harrison ave	Mrs. Geo F Jones
Josephs, Lyman C	New York		Purgatory road	
King, Mrs Delancy	New York		Sunnyside Place	
King, Woodbury	New York		Sunnyside Place	
Kernoys, Mrs Edward	New York	King Cottage	Bellevue ave, opp Perry	at LeRoy King
Kernochan J P	New York	Sea View	Marine st	
Ketchum, Mrs Eugene	New York		Webster & Spring st	
Kidd, George W	New York	Clover Patch	65 Narragansett ave	W. D. King
Kilburn, Lieut W	U. S. N.	Babcock Villa	Dellton ave	Mrs. M. C. Babcock
King, Mrs Edward	New York		Spring & Bowery st	
King, LeRoy	New York		Bellevue & Berkely aves	
Knower, John	New York	Net Cliff	Bellevue ave & Cliffs	
Knowlton, F P	Brooklyn	Torrance Cottage	Bellevue ave	Mrs. D. Torrance E.
Knowlton, F J	Brooklyn	Woolsey Villa	Rhode Island ave	Miss S. C. Woolsey

Name	City	Cottage	Location	Owner
Lawrence, Henry S	New York	Doni Cottage	Catherine ave. & Bath road	Mrs. Worcester
Lawrence, Prescott	New York	Edna House	Lafayette ave.	D. King
Leary, Arthur	New York	Paul Cottage	De Wolf st.	A. G. Paul, Est.
Ledyard L. C	New York	Cottage XX	Easton's Beach	Newport Land Trust Co.
Lee, Dr. Charles Carroll	New York	Sargent Villa	Kay st.	Mrs. L. S. Sargent
Leech, J. F.	Brooklyn	Willmerdoe Villa	Bonniecrest Hill	S. H. Willmerdoe
Leroy, Mrs. Daniel	New York		42 Bellevue ave.	
LeRoy, Stuyvesant	New York		4, Malbone	
Livermore, Mrs. C. F	New York	Inchiquin	Bellevue ave. & Ledge road	
Livermore, Maj. W. R	U. S. A.	Little Cottage	Everett Place	W. McC. Little
Lorillard Louis L.	New York	Vinland	on her point ave. & Cliffs	
Low, Abiel A	Brooklyn	Sunset Lodge	Harrison road Castle Hill	
Low, A Augustus	Brooklyn	Sunset Lodge	Harrison road Castle Hill	A A Low
Low, Josiah O	Brooklyn	Broadlawn	Harrison road Castle Hill	
Lush, Dr. W. T	New York	Griswold Villa	Bellevue ave. opp. Temple	U. S. A. Griswold
Luther, Charles F	Fall River	Bateman's	Bateman's Point	
Mahony, John H	New York		Bellevue & Lake View ave	
Marquand, Henry G	New York	Linden Gate	K'y ave. & Ocean ave sts	
Mason, Miss Ellen F	Boston		K'y ave. & Bath road	
Mason, Mrs. C. C	New York		43 Everett Place	
Mason, J. Griffith	New York		43 Everett Place	
Matthews, Mrs. Mary	New York	Steven's Villa	Berkeley ave	Mrs. Esran Stevens
McAslister, Ward	New York	Lyman Cottage	LeRoy ave.	Est. C. Lyman
McClung, Louis D	New York	Jones' Villa	Rose cliff ave. & Cliffs	Miss C. O. Jones
McKay, Gordon	New York		Marine ave	
McVickar, Henry G	New York	Walsh	Catherine st. & Gibbs ave	Dr. J. J. Mason
Merrill, Mrs. George	New York	Cozy Nook	Bellevue ave. n' Narragan't	
Miller, George M	New York	Rock Mere	Bellevue ave. & Ledge road	
Miller, H. Ray	New York		Bellevue ave. n' Webster st	
Miller, William St.	New York		Bellevue ave. & Webster st	
Mills, Ogden	New York		Bellevue ave. & Cliffs	
Mitchell, Mary A	New York		43 Church st	
Moran, Theodore T	New York	Halidon Hall	Wellington ave	Mrs. L. V. Harishorn
Morgan, E. D	New York	Beacon Rock	Brenton Cove, Harrison av	
Morgan, Miss	New York	Snug Harbor	Bath road ave.	Mrs. C. H. Baldwin
Moore, Clement C	New York	Bell's cottage	Catherine st. & Gibbs ave	Mrs. J. A. DuBois
Morris, Miss Hannah	Philadelphia		80 Washington st	
Morris, Mrs. J. H	Georgetown	Maitland Cottage	Cypresses' end of Second st	
Morris, Miss Jane	Philadelphia		80 Washington st	
Morris, J Stokes	Philadelphia	Maitland Cottage	Cypress' end of Second st	
Morris, Mrs. B. H	Philadelphia	Allbesi Cottage	Chestnut st	
Morse, F. Rollins	New York	Brown Villa	Bellevue ave. op. LeRoy av	Mrs. M. A. P. Brown
Mortimer, Stanley	New York		Rhode Island ave	R. J. Arnold
Mott, Thomas	Philadelphia	Rotherford Villa	Harrison ave	S. Rotherford
Neill, Edward M			Brack Street	
Norman, George H	Boston	Belair	Greenough place and Divine Vista st	
O'Brien, John	New York	Inchiquin	Bellevue av and Ledge road	
Oelrichs, Charles M	New York	Forsyth's Cottage	88 Ayrault st	Russell Forsyth
Ogden, Francis L.	New York	Maple Shade	Red Cross ave. and Buena Vista st	
Ogden, Mrs. J. D	New York	Maple Shade	Red Cross av. and Buena Vista st	
Ogden, Mrs. W. B	New York	Carley Villa	Bellevue av., opp. Perry st	G. G. Haven.
Osgood, William H	New York		Bellevue & Narragansett ave	
Parkman, George F.	Boston		Bellevue ave. and Cliffs	
Pannecote, Sir Julian	Washington	Carey Cottage	13 Bath road	Mrs. Emily Carey.
Pearson, Mrs. Frederic	New York		Russell's ave. Ochre Point	
Peckham, Walter R	New York		Ocean House	
Pell, John B.	Brooklyn	Marrion Cottage	Purse dry road	
Pepper, Dr. David	Philadelphia		11 Greenough place	
Pepper, Mrs. S	Philadelphia		11 Greenough place	
Perkins, Mrs. C. C	Boston	Brown Villa	Bellevue ave. opp. LeRoy av	
Perkins, Capt. G. H	Boston	De Rham Cottage	Bellevue av	W. G. Weld
Perrine, Dr. James	Montreal		Ocean House	
Phinney, Theodore W	New York	Hilltop	Kingstown & Carroll ave	
Pierson, Gen. J. Fred	New York		Bellevue av., near Ledge rd	
Pinard, Charles	New York	Clover Nook	5 Annandale road	
Popham, S. B	Philadelphia	Maitland Cottage	Cypress st., end of Second	
Potter, D. C	Boston	Leavitt Cottage	81 Pelham st	A. L. Leavitt.
Post, Miss Laura J	New York		64 Thurston ave	Barnes Baker
Post, William	New York		Bellevue av., near Ruggles	
Potter, Edward T	New York		2 Catherine st	
Potter, Mrs. H. C	New York		Rhode Island ave	
Potter, Julian	New York		21 Catherine st	
Powell, Dr. Samuel G	New York	The Anchorage	18 Beach st	
Pratt, H. Ruthven	New York	Stevens Villa	Berkeley ave	Mrs. Esran Stevens.
Pratt, Samuel F	Boston	Birds' Nest	45 Bellevue ave	
Prince, Col. W. F., U. S. A	Boston		Beach View ave	
Read, William G	New York		Ocean House	
Redmond, Gould H	New York	The Berkley	John st. & Bellevue ave	
Remsen, F. E	Brooklyn	Maitland Cottage	Cypress av., end of 2d st	
Rhinelander, F. W	New York		10 Redwood st	
Rice, Henry A	Boston	Bay Bank	Washington st	
Rider, W. H	Bangor	Maitland Cottage	Cypress st., end of 2d st	
Rives, Arthur L	New York		7 Red Cross av	
Rives, Mrs. G. L.	New York	Swanhurst	Bellevue av	Mrs. S. S. Whiting
Rives, Dr. Wm. C	New York		Red Cross ave & Bath road	
Robbins, Henry A	New York	Walsh	Catherine st & Gibbs ave	Dr. J. J. Mason
Robinson, Dr. Beverley	New York	Pennington Cottage	Parker ave. & Clay st	G. H. Warren
Rogers, Archibald	New York	The Ledges	Ocean ave	R. M. Cushing
Rogers, Mrs. William H	Boston	Morning Side	Gibbs ave	
Rook, Mrs. Edward F	New York	Jay Cottage	Buena Vista st	Augustus Jay
Rose, Rowland L	Providence	Swift Cottage	Wheatland & Bellevue ave.	Swift Estate
Ruthven, Mrs. C. V	New York	Warden Cottage	88 Ayrault st.	Mrs. Admiral Reed Werden
Sands, Andrew H	New York		Ocean House	
Sands, Mrs. A. L	New York		Greenough place and Catherine st	
Sanford, Mrs. Milton H	New York	Eden Villa	73 Washington st.	
Satterlee, Dr. F. LeRoy	New York	The Innes	12 Clay st	
Schmerhorn, W. C	New York	Pinard's Cottage No 2	Narragansett ave.	C. & J. A. Pinard
Sheldon, Frederic	New York		Annandale road and Narragansett ave	
Sherman, Mrs. S. H	Wilmington, Del.	Maitland Cottage	Cypress, end of Second st	
Sherman, Wm. Watts	New York		Victoria and Shepard aves	
Shimamina, Mrs.	Boston	Muenchinger's	Bellevue ave.	
Sloane, Henry T.	New York	Duchess De Dino Villa	Bellevue av and Bowery st	Duchess De Dino
Smith, Benjamin R.	Philadelphia		64 Washington st	
Sorchan, Victor	New York	Vose Cottage	4 Bath road	W. S. Vose
Sorzano, Mme. A. I	New York	Neilson Cottage	30 Cottage st	Miss Neilson
Spaulding, A. W	New York		LeRoy ave	J. M. Hodgson
Spencer, J. Thompson	Philadelphia		Ruggles ave	
Spencer, Lorillard	New York	The Moorings	Harrison ave.	Mrs. S. Hamilton
Squire, Newton	New York		Ocean House	

Stanard, Mrs. Martha...... Virginia .... 37 Bull st. .... *
Steedman, Mrs .... New York .... Bruen Villino .... Bellevue, opp. LeRoy av.... Mrs M A D Bruen
Stevens, P. W............ New York .... Rosevale .... Narragansett ave .... Estate C. H. Russell.
Stevens, J. A .... New York .... 73 Rhode Island av ...... *
Stevens, Mrs. Paran ..... New York .... Marietta Villa .... Bellevue and Jones aves ... *
Stewart, Jr. John A ..... New York .... Kane Cottage .... Bellevue ave. .... W. L. Kane.
Stitt, Seth B........... Philadelphia ...... Park Gate. .... Pelham st., opp. Touro Pk .. *
Stockton, Lt. Comdr C B .. U. S. N .... Swinburne Cottage ... Greenough place .... Hn D.T. Swinburne.
Stockton, Mrs. Mary A .... Boston .... Bellevue av. & Bellevue ct .. *
Stoker, Anson Phelps ..... New York .... Craig Mere .... Beacon Hill, Harrison av ... J. H. Glover.
Stone, Mrs Joseph F ...... New York .... Bellevue ave & Webster st. .. *
Stuart, Ronald A .... Boston .... Ocean House .... *
Swan, J A .... Columbus, O .... 84 Kay st .... C. M. Oelrichs.
Swan, Mrs S. Turner ..... Baltimore .... Wayside. .... Bellevue ave & Bellevue ct .. *
Taggart, Philip S .... New York .... Maplecote .... Broadway .... *
Tailor, Edward S .... New York .... Shields Villa .... Ruggles ave .... C. W. Shields.
Taylor Henry A. C .... New York .... Annandale road .... *
Thayer, Nathaniel .... Boston .... Bellevue av & Cliffs .... *
Thorn, Mrs. W. K .... New York .... Stoneleigh. .... Narragansett av.&Spring st .. *
Throop, Beverest .... Bysmpeque .... Bellevue ave .... *
Tucker, E. G .... New York .... Rose Cottage .... Beach st. & Greenough pl'ce . *
Tucker, G. M .... New York .... Kay cor of Pine u st .... *
Trapp, John E. .... Providence .... Ocean House .... *
Turie Tustin, Joseph ..... New York .... 142 Mill st .... *
Tweedy, Edmund .... Newport .... 20 Berkshire Court. ..... *
Tyler, George J .... Philadelphia .... 77 Bellevue Court. ..... *
Tyler, H. D .... Philadelphia .... 17 Bellevue Court ...... *
Van Alen, J. J .... New York .... Wakehurst .... Ochre Point .... *
Van Brunt, Mrs .... Brooklyn .... One mile corner. .... *
Vanderbilt, F. W .... New York .... Rough Point .... Bellevue ave. & Cliffs .... *
Vanderbilt, William K .... New York .... Hunnewell Cottage .... Yznaga ave & Cliffs ...... Hunnewell estate
Vanderbilt, William K .... New York .... Wales Cottage .... Yznaga ave & Cliffs ...... G. W. Wales
Van Santvoord, Alfred .... New York .... Washington St. .... T. A. Havemeyer.
Van Smith, Mrs J .... Baltimore .... Bateman's. .... Bateman's Point. .... *
Walker, Mrs & Miss ...... Norfolk, Va .... Ocean House. .... *
Wallace, Mrs J. W .... Philadelphia ...... Spencer Villa .... Ruggles ave .... *
Warren, George H. .... New York .... 6 Narragansett ave. ..... *
Warren, S. Whitney ...... New York .... 4 Kay st .... *
Watson, Dr W. Argyle .... New York .... 2 Spring st .... *
Webster, Sidney .... New York .... Lyndenhurst .... Bellevue ave. .... J. M. Hodgson.
Webster, Hamilton F ..... New York .... Lyndenhurst .... Bellevue ave. .... *
Weld, George W .... Boston .... Weld Lodge .... 84 Narragansett ave. .... *
Weld, William F .... Boston .... Weld Lodge .... 84 Narragansett ave .... *
Weld, William G .... Boston .... Bellevue ave n. Parker ave. . *
Weld, Mrs W. F .... Boston .... Weld Lodge .... 84 Narragansett ave. .... *
Wells, Wm. Starrs ...... New York .... Pansy Cottage .... Bellevue & Ruggles aves. .. *
Wharton, Edward R .... New York .... Pen Craig .... Harrison ave .... Mrs G. F. Jones.
Wheeler, Miss J. B ...... Philadelphia ...... Shore Cottage .... Washington st .... *
Whistler, Mrs. Jos. S .... Baltimore .... Shamrock Cliff ...... Ridge Road, Castle Hill. ... G. M. Hulton.
Whitdey, Thomas D. ...... Baltimore .... Bateman's. .... Bateman's Point. .... *
White, Mrs. M. B .... New York .... Ocean House .... *
White-house, W. F ...... New York .... Eastbourne Lodge. .... Rhode Island ave .... *
Whiting, Augustus ...... New York .... Seabhurst .... Bellevue ave & Webster st . Mrs. S. & Whiting.
Whiting, Mrs. S. S ...... New York .... Seabhurst .... Bellevue ave & Webster st. .. *
Whitney, D. A .... Boston .... Maitland Cottage .... Cypress st., end of 2d st .... *
Whitney, Mrs F. T ...... Fikton Md .... Bateman's. .... Bateman's Point......... *
Whitney, William C ...... New York .... Travers Villa ...... 26 Narragansett ave ..... Mrs M. L. Travers.
Whittridge, John C ...... Baltimore .... Sandy Point, east shore... *
Whitwort, S. Horatio .... Boston .... 17 Berkeley ave .... *
Williams, J. P .... New York .... Ocean House. .... *
Williamson, Richard ..... Philadelphia ...... Biggs' Cottage ...... 26 Catherine st. .... *
Willing, Edward S ...... Philadelphia .... Webster and Spring sts.... *
Willing, Richard L. ..... Philadelphia .... 2 Red Cross ave. ...... *
Willoughby, Hugh L. ..... Philadelphia ...... The Chalet .... Halidon ave .... *
Wilson, Prof Jas Hazard .. New York .... Coddington Point ...... *
Wilson, M. Orme .... New York .... Bienvenue .... 97 Narragansett ave ..... *
Wilson, Richard T ...... New York .... Bienvenue .... 97 Narragansett ave .... *
Wilson, W. E .... Boston .... Ocean House .... *
Winthrop, Buchanan ...... New York .... Pinard Cottage No. 3 .. Narragansett ave .... C. & J. A. Pinard.
Winthrop, Everton L. ..... New York .... Bellevue ave .... *
Wister William .... Germantown .... Maitland Cottage ..... Cypress st., end of Second. .. *
Witcher, Mrs. E. A ...... Jersey City .... Maitland Cottage ..... Cypress st, end of Second. .. *
Witherbee, Mrs. Silas H .. New York .... Bonytson Hill .... *
Wolfe, Joel B .... New York .... Hall Cottage .... Bellevue ave .... Peley Hall.
Wyman, John J .... New York .... Graystone .... Ochre Point ave .... *
Zabriskie, Andrew C...... New York .... Zabriskie House ...... Rhode Island ave and Cath-
....erine st .... *
Zabriskie, Lansing ...... New York .... 86 Rhode Island ave ..... *

OFFICERS STATIONED AT FORT ADAMS.

Colonel .... John Mendenhall, in command of Post —, 2d Art.
Surgeon .... Maj Henry Lippencott.
Asst. Surgeon .... Capt A W Taylor
Adj, Rec & Post .... 1st Lieut. W. A Simpson, ... 2d Art.
Q'm'r, Rec & Post .... 1st " T. M. Weaver, Jr. .... 2d Art.

Major ...... Harry C. Cushing, Light Battery, 4th Art.   Captain ...... George Mitchell, Co. G, 2d Art.
1st Lieut ... H. E. Anderson, ... " " "   1st Lieut .... Loomis Niles, ... " "
1st " ...... W S Alexander, ... " " "   1st " ...... S. Bodman, ... " "
2d " ...... W. Bodman, ... " " "   2d " ...... J. S. Lewis, ... " "
Captain ...... Louis V Caziarc, Co. C, 2d Art.   Captain ...... Frank C. Grugan, Co. H, 2d Art.
1st Lieut .... Sedree Smith, ... " "   1st Lieut ... M. Crawford, ... " "
1st " ...... G. F. E. Harrison, ... " "   2d " ...... Chas F. Parker, ... " "
2d " ...... O. W. Ketcham, ... " "

OFFICE OF THE U. S. NAVAL TRAINING STATION.

Captain............................Francis M. Bunce.   Surgeon.........................Charles A. Siegfried
Lieut. Comdr.......................Edwin Longnecker.   Asst. Surgeon...................Charles H. T. Lowndes
Lieutenant.........................William Kilburn   ....Robert M. Kennedy.
...................................Florence S. Prime.   Paymaster.......................John Convine
Ensign.............................Lewis J. Clark   Chief Engineer..................David P Jones.
Chaplain...........................W O Holway.   1st Lieut, Marine Corps.........Randolph Dickins.

OFFICERS OF THE U. S. TORPEDO STATION.

Commander .... Theodore F. Jewell.   Lieut.....................W. B. Marshall.
Lieut. Comdr. .... H W Lyon.   Surgeon...................P. Fitzsimmons
....   P. A. Paymaster...........T. J. Cowie
Lieut......................... T C McLean.   Professor.................C. E. Munroe.
.... M. F. Hall.

CHURCH DIRECTORY.

PROTESTANT EPISCOPAL.

Trinity Parish, Rev. George J. Magill, rector. Holy Communion every Sunday morning at 7 o'clock in Kay Chapel; morning service at 11 o'clock; evening service at 7 o'clock in Trinity Church. Service for Scandinavians at 8:45 a. m. in Kay Chapel. Sunday school at 9:30 a. m.

All Saints' Memorial, corner Beach and Cottage streets. Morning service at 11 o'clock, evening service at 7 o'clock.

St. George's Chapel, Rhode Island avenue, Rev. C. C. Gilliat, D. D. Holy Communion every Sunday morning at 8 o'clock. Morning service at 11 o'clock, evening service at 7 o'clock.

Chapel of St. John, the Evangelist Poplar street. Rev. F. L. Buckey. Holy Communion every Sunday morning at 7 o'clock. Morning service at 10 o'clock, evening service at 6 o'clock.

Emmanuel Church, Spring street, Rev. H. H. Potter, rector. Morning service at 11 o'clock, evening service at 7:30 o'clock. Holy Communion first Sunday in each month at 11 o'clock a. m. and on third Sunday at 7 a. m.

St. Mary's Parish, South Portsmouth, R. I., Rev. G. H. Patterson, rector. Morning service at 11 o'clock.

St. Columba's Berkeley Memorial Church, near Indian avenue, Middletown, R. I., Rev. J. H. Diman, morning service at 11 o'clock, evening service at 4 o'clock.

METHODIST EPISCOPAL.

First Church, Marlborough street. Rev. W. A. Luce, pastor. Sermon at 10:30 a. m. except first Sunday of the month. Holy Communion first Sunday of each month at 10:30 a. m. Sermon at 7:30 p. m. first Sunday of each month. Sunday school at 2:30 p. m.

Thames Street Church, Rev. G. W. Hunt, pastor. Prayer meeting at 9:30 a. m. Sunday school at 10:30 a. m., sermon at 3 p. m., evening service at 7:30 p. m.

Middletown Four Corners, Rev. J. F. Cooper, pastor. Sunday school at 10:30 a. m., preaching at 3 p. m., evening meeting at 7:30 p. m.

Swedish Mission, Annandale road, Rev. H. Olsen. Services at 10:45 a. m. and 2:45 p. m.

Mount Zion (colored), Bellevue avenue, Rev. W. H. H. Butler, pastor. Services at 10:30 a. m. and 3 p. m. Sunday school at 1:30 p. m.

BAPTIST.

First Church, Spring street, Rev. E. P. Tuller, pastor. Sermon at 10:30 a. m., and 7:30 p. m. Bible service at 12 m.

Second Church, North Baptist street, Rev. S. W. Stevens, pastor. Sunday school at 2:30 a. m., sermon at 3 and 7:30 p. m.

Central Church, Clarke street, Rev. W. Randolph, pastor. Morning service at 10:30, evening service at 7:30. Sunday school at 12 m.

Shiloh Church, corner Mary and School streets, Rev. H. N. Jeter, pastor. Morning service at 11, evening service at 7:30.

CONGREGATIONAL.

United Church, Spring street, corner Pelham. Rev. F. P. Emerson, pastor. Morning service at 11. Sunday school at 12:15 p. m.

Union Church (colored), Division street, Rev. M. VanHorne, pastor. Sermon at 3 and 7:30 p. m. Sunday school at 1 p. m.

PRESBYTERIAN.

First Church, Grace Chapel, Wellington avenue. Rev. J. M. Craig, pastor. Preaching at 10:30 a. m. Sunday school at 12 p. m., evening service at 7:30 p. m.

St. Mary's ....
Rev. ....
Low ....

St. .... D. .... Rev. .... at

JEWS.

Synagogue, Touro street, Rev. A. P. Mendes, rabbi. Sabbath eve service on Fridays at 7 p. m. Sabbath morn service on Saturdays at 9 a. m. Bible class on Sundays at 10 a. m.

UNITARIAN.

Channing Memorial Church, Pelham street, opposite Touro Park. Rev. G. W. Cutler, minister. Morning service at 11 a. m. Sunday school at 12 noon.

FRIENDS.

Meeting House, Marlborough street. Morning service at 10:30. Evening service at 7. First-day school at 12 noon.

At the U. S. N. Training Station, Coasters Harbor Island, services are held by Rev. W. C. Holway, chaplain at 10:30 a. m.

TABLE OF DISTANCES TO PROMINENT PLACES.

	Miles
Washington square to Ocean	
Easton's Beach	
Sachuest Beach	
Third Beach	
Purgatory	
Hanging Rocks	
Touro Park to Bailey's Beach	
Touro Park to and around Ocean Drive back to Washington square	
Along cliffs from Bath road to Forty Steps	
Marine avenue	
Bailey's Beach	
Glen via beaches, Indian ave. and East road	
From Mile Corner to Butt's Hill via East Road	
From Mile Corner to Prescott's Headquarters, Portsmouth via West road	
Bellevue ave. to Easton's Beach	
From Forty Steps to Easton's Point by water	
From Forty Steps to Sachuest Point by water	
From Rammister's wharf to Fort Adams by water	
From Rammister's Wharf to Torpedo Station by water	
Thames street to Fort Greene via Long Wharf and Washington street	
Newport to Jamestown	
Ferry landing to Beaver Tail	
Ferry landing to Fort Dumpling	
East to West Ferry	
Beaver Tail to entrance to Conanicut Park	

THE HOURS OF ADMISSION TO PLACES OF INTEREST.

Newport Artillery Armory, Clarke street, daily.

Redwood Library, Bellevue avenue, 10 a. m. to 2 p. m.

People's Library, 360 Thames street, 10 a. m. to 5:30 p. m.

Easton's Beach, bathing for both sexes until 11 p. m. and after 2 p. m. For men only from 11 to 2 p. m.

Historical Society Rooms, Touro street, 10 a. m. to 2 p. m.

Natural History Society Rooms, Touro street, 10 a. m. to 2 p. m.

Trinity Church, Church street entrance, can be had by applying at No. 95 Church street for key.

Casino, Bellevue avenue. Morning concert 10 a. m. to 1:30 p. m. Music and dancing Mondays and Fridays, evening, from 8:30 p. m. to 11:30 p. m. Sunday evening music from 8 to 11. Admission to morning concert 50 cents. Music and dancing $1.00. At other times 25 cents.

U. S. Naval Training Station, Coasters Harbor Island, from 1 p. m. until sunset.

Fort Adams, guard mount and dress parade 11 a. m. daily except Saturday and Sunday.

TIDE TABLE.

	JULY		AUG		SEPT.		OCT.	
	A. M.	P. M.	A. M.	P. M.	A. M.	P. M.	A. M.	P. M.
1	3 14	3 25	3 45	4 42	5 51	5 52	5 51	6 13
2	4 07	4 15	4 12	5 29	6 25	6 29	6 16	6 43
3	4 55	4 55	5 15	6 06	6 55	7 06	6 43	7 12
4	5 41	5 37	6 52	6 46	7 23	7 41	7 14	7 43
5	6 26	6 14	7 27	7 24	7 55	8 15	7 49	8 19
6	7 10	7 04	8 21	9 06	8 34	8 52	8 30	9 01
7	7 55	7 24	9 22	8 41	9 12	9 35	9 18	9 55
8	8 41	8 25	10 22	......	9 55	10 25	10 14	11 03
9	9 31	9 19	10 51	......	10 51	11 26	11 20	....
10	10 21	11 00	......	11 00	11 51	....	0 21	12 30
11	11 11	11 09	11 11	....	0 37	12 59	1 34	1 40
12	11 52	......	1 13	12 39	1 47	2 02	2 31	2 44
13	0 07	12 15	1 11	1 34	2 45	3 01	3 21	3 40
14	0 41	1 12	2 40	2 30	3 44	3 55	4 05	4 31
15	1 57	2 15	3 25	3 21	4 25	4 45	4 54	5 20
16	2 47	3 01	4 50	4 11	5 14	5 35	5 44	6 06
17	3 32	3 44	4 25	5 00	5 50	6 24	6 17	6 53
18	4 17	4 28	5 12	5 49	6 44	7 12	7 03	7 41
19	5 02	5 14	6 00	6 37	7 11	8 02	7 45	8 34
20	5 47	6 00	6 52	7 28	8 19	8 55	8 38	9 32
21	6 36	6 49	7 52	8 21	9 10	10 53	9 34	10 38
22	7 25	7 41	8 35	9 16	10 02	...0 58	10 34	11 53
23	8 24	8 36	9 45	10 15	11 04	....	11 41	....
24	9 22	9 35	10 22	11 20	0 10	0 15	1 10	0 52
25	10 20	10 38	11 11	....	1 27	1 32	2 15	2 00
26	11 18	11 42	0 11	0 47	2 35	2 36	3 06	2 59
27	......	0 15	1 11	1 91	3 32	3 24	3 47	3 51
28	0 50	1 19	2 17	2 45	4 17	4 13	4 19	4 38
29	1 56	2 15	3 55	3 42	4 55	4 57	4 44	5 15
30	2 55	3 04	4 55	4 30	5 26	5 37	5 11	5 46
31	3 54	3 46	5 55	5 44			5 37	6 12

ADDENDA:

Names of Summer Residents Arriving Too Late for Insertion in Regular Or...

Beach, F O	New York		Casino Club		
Buckney, Newton	New Orleans	Deas villa	Easton's Pond	Mrs Z C Deas	
Cole, Hugh L	New York	Stonacre	Bellevue and Victoria ave	J W Ellis	
De Heredia, C	New York	Seaverse	Bellevue ave and Cliffs	H H Cook	
Ellis, W D	New York	Cliff Hotel	Cliff View ave		
Ellis, Ralph N	New York	Stonacre	Bellevue and Victoria ave		
French T Amos	New York	Harbor View	Chastellux ave		
Jones, Mason Renshaw	New York	Bay View	Halidon ave		
Le Rouls, Rene de la Ville	Paris		6 Bath road		
Lanier, J F D	New York	Eldredge villa	Ruggles ave		
Lewis, J Nelson	Philadelphia	Fadden cottage	2 Bath road		
Noble, J M	Boston	Wales cottage	Yznaga ave	G W Wales	
O'Conor, John C	New York	Baker cottage	40 Cranston ave	Darius Baker	
Ronalds, P Lorillard, Jr	New York		5 Bath road		
Ryttenberg, M G	New York	Hotel Aquidneck	Pelham st		
Stuart, Clinton	New York	Fadden cottage	2 Bath road		
Steele, S Sedgwick	Hartford	Conkling cottage	Touro Park, West		
Shaw, Philander	Brooklyn		16 Touro st		
Schiedt, J A	Germantown, Pa	Clifton House	Bellevue ave		
Von Wulffen, Hans	Washington	Reitz cottage	14 John st		
Van Arsdale, R M	New York	Cliff Hotel	Cliff View ave		
Wetmore, Geo Peabody		Chateau-sur-mer	Bellevue ave		
Wetmore, Mrs Samuel	New York		Bellevue ave		

· GEORGE H. CARR ·

Bookseller and Stationer,

ENGLISH, FRENCH AND AMERICAN STATIONERY.

Card Plates and Card Engraving.

Playing Cards.   Picture Framing.

Stylographic and Fountain Pens.

IMPORTED ·:· TISSUE ·:· PAPERS.

172 THAMES STREET.

CARRY BROS, ??

DEALERS IN

Staple and Fancy Groceries, Fish,

Foreign and Domestic

Fruit

And Every Kind of Early Produce in Their Season.

257 & 259 THAMES ST.,
NEWPORT. R. I.

J. J. CARRY.

CLIFTON

HOUSE,

BELLEVUE AVENUE.

**One of the Pleasantest Cafes
in the City Connected
with the House.**

TERMS REASONABE.

R. F. CUMMINGS. PROP.

Newport Transfer Company.

GENERAL BAGGAGE EXPRESS.

Messengers of the Company will be found on the incoming trains of the Old Colony Railroad and the boats of the Fall River, Worcester and Providence Lines.

TICKETS FOR THE ABOVE LINES ARE ON SALE AT OUR OFFICE

Calls will be promptly made at any part of the city and baggage checked at residences to Boston, New York, Philadelphia, Baltimore, Washington and other principal cities.

This feature saves the traveller being obliged to go to trains and boats at an early hour, or to arrange for identification or checking of his baggage.

All shipments consigned to the care of the Transfer Express Company will receive prompt attention.

Office 30 Bellevue Ave., 272 Thames St. and New York Freight Depot, Fall River Line.

A. P. BRYANT, Pres.,

E. B. HARRINGTON, Treasurer and Manager.

M. F. COTTRELL,

NO. 8 TRAVERS BLOCK,

Importer of Fine Millinery.

MOURNING GOODS

A Specialty.

T. MUMFORD SEABURY,

DEALER IN

BOOTS

&

SHOES

134 THAMES ST.,

NEWPORT. R. I.

NEW NO. 214.

PHOTOGRAPHS.

Souvenir Novelties and Albums.

⇥⊹ Views of Newport ⊹⇤

AND VICINITY.

A Complete Line of Popular Novels at Lowest Cut Rates,

For Sale by

NEW YORK BOOK CO.,

142 THAMES STREET.

We Also Have a Line of

FINE STATIONERY,

ALBUMS,

PHOTOGRAPH FRAMES,

Standard Books,

⇥⊹ BIBLES, ⊹⇤

Prayer Books,

And Other Goods Usually Found at a Stationer's.

ESTABLISHED 1866.

A. SCHMIDT & SON,

Travers Block, - Newport, R. I.

AND

347 Fifth avenue, between 33d and 34th Streets,

NEW YORK.

IMPORTERS

AND

DECORATORS

Of Choice Grades of

PORCELAINS, BRIC-A-BRAC, ETC.

Orders taken for importations for special decorations in all kinds
of table ware.

NEW YORK,

302 Fifth Avenue.

GOBELIN AND BEAUVAIS

TAPESTRIES.

LOUIS XV. LOUIS XVI.

FURNITURE.

ORIENTAL AND EUROPEAN

PORCELAINS.

FINE

OLD ENGLISH

SILVER.

DUVEEN BROTHERS.

108 AND 110 BELLEVUE AVE., NEWPORT, R. I.

FLEMISH

AND

ARRAS

TAPESTRIES.

Fine Carved Woodwork

of the

ITALIAN AND FLEMISH

RENAISSANCE PERIODS.

LONDON,

181 OXFORD ST.

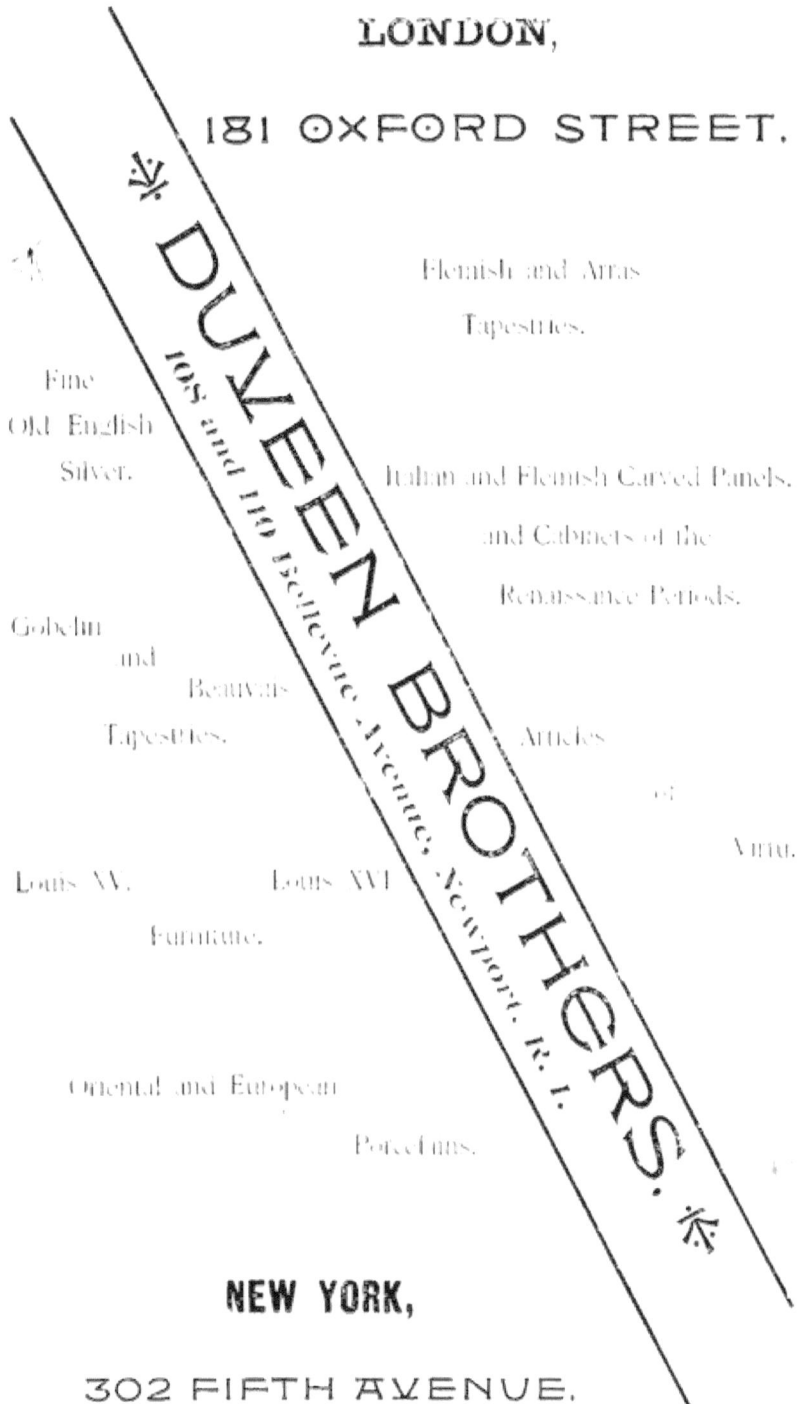

HOWARD & CO.

PRECIOUS STONES

FINE
JEWELRY

Modern and Antique
Silver.

---

264 Fifth Avenue.

Bellevue Avenue, Newport.

67 Regent Street, London.

37 Avenue de l'Opera, Paris.

F. P. GARRETTSON & CO.,

DEALERS IN

Fine Wines, Teas, Coffees and Choice Groceries,

16 AND 20 WASHINGTON SQUARE,

NEWPORT, R. I.

118 AND 156 FRONT STREET,
NEW YORK.

Specimen Prices of Standard Groceries.

Please Compare with those You are Now Paying.

21 lbs. Standard Granulated Sugar, $1.00.

Java and Mocha, 35 cts. per lb.

An excellent Tea, 35 cts. per lb.

10 lbs. $3.00. With case, $3.50.

20 " $6.60 with case.

By the chest, 29 cts. per lb. less 5 per cent., which virtually reduces the same to less than 28 cts. per lb. Samples sent on application.

McCann's Irish Oatmeal, $1.40 per tin.

Very best Rice, 9 to 11 cts.

Imperial Granum, 90 and 50 cts.

Eagle Brand Condensed Milk, 16 cts.

Cox's Gelatine, 14 cts.

Van Houten's Cocoa, 90, 50 and 25 cts.

Raisins, cooking, 11 cts.

" very best, 15 cts.

Prunes, 11 cts. and 20 cts.

Naphey's Lard, 5 lb. tins, 60 cts.

" " 10 lb. tins, $1.20

Macaroni, etc., 12 to 15 cts.

Olive Oil, B & G and others, 75 cts. per bottle, $7.50 per case.

Best French Peas, 35 cts. Per dozen, $3.50.

" Mushrooms, 35 cts. " " "

Franco-American Soups, average price, 35 cts.

Tomatoes, 10, 12 and 15 cts. per tin.

Corn, 12, 15 and 18 cts. per tin.

Canned Fruits, 28 and 35 cts. per tin.

C & B Jams, 17 to 22 cts. per jar.

Colgate's Laundry Soap, $6.25 per box.

Salt for cooking, 15 cts. per bag.

Household Ammonia, 12 cts. per bottle.

Duryea's & Kingsford's Starch, 50 cts. per box.

Star Mills Toilet Paper, 25 cts. per package.

Rising Sun Stove Polish, 5 cts. " "

Sapolio, 3 cakes, 25 cts.

Alcohol 96 degrees, 75 cts. per bottle.

Knickerbocker Beer, per dozen, $1.00.

C & C Ginger Ale, per dozen, $1.50.

Nicholson's Liquid Bread, per dozen, $3.00.

Apollinaris, quarts, per dozen, $2.00.

" pints, " " $1.50

Clysmic, quarts, " " $2.00

" pints, " " $1.50

Wines, Clarets, Champagnes, Sherries, etc., sold at the prices given in the Price Lists of the two leading Grocery Houses in New York City. A further discount is given in 5 case lots.

We wish to show by this list of sundries, that by purchasing in Newport of us, you save the trouble of sending away for your goods, cost of transportation and any goods that may be damaged or imperfect are at once replaced. In short it is a mutual benefit.